HOLY COW

Elsie Bovary is a cow, and a pretty happy one at that. But a glimpse of something called an "industrial meat farm" shakes her understanding of the world to its core, and she decides to escape to a better, safer place. A motley crew is formed: Elsie; Shalom, a grumpy pig; and Tom, a suave turkey who can't fly but can work tolen pass and slapdash human disguises, they head for the airport . . .

HOLY COW

DAVID DUCHOVNY

ISIS
LARGE
PRINT

First published in Great Britain 2015
by
Headline Publishing Group

First Isis Edition
published 2018
by arrangement with
Headline Publishing Group
An Hachette UK Company

A catalogue record for this book is available
from the British Library.

ISBN 978–1–78541–595–1 (hb)
ISBN 978–1–78541–601–9 (pb)

Published by
F. A. Thorpe (Publishing)
Anstey, Leicestershire

Set by Words & Graphics Ltd.
Anstey, Leicestershire
Printed and bound in Great Britain by
T. J. International Ltd., Padstow, Cornwall

This book is printed on acid-free paper

For West and Miller

*And Blue and George and Black and Joe
and Patty and Delilah*

The difference in mind between man and the higher animals, great as it is, certainly is one of degree and not of kind.

— CHARLES DARWIN

CHAPTER
ONE

PLEASE ALLOW ME TO INTRODUCE MYSELF

Most people think cows can't think. Hello. Let me rephrase that, most people think cows can't think, and have no feelings. Hello, again. I'm a cow, my name is Elsie, yes, I know. And that's no bull. See? We can think, feel, and joke, most of us anyway. My great-aunt Elsie, whom I'm named after, has no sense of humor. At all. I mean zero. She doesn't even like jokes with humans in them doing stupid things. Like that one that goes — two humans walk into a barn . . . Wait, I may not have much time here, I can't mess around.

Just trying to get certain things out of the way. Let's see, oh yeah, how am I writing this, you may wonder, when I have no fingers? Can't hold a pen. Believe me, I've tried. Not pretty. Not that there are many pens around anymore, what with all the computers. And even though we can think and feel and be funny, we cannot speak. At least to humans. We have what you people used to call an "oral tradition." Stories and wisdom are handed down from mother cow to daughter calf, from generation to generation. Much the way you receive your *Odysseys* or your *Iliads*. Singing, even. Sorry for the name-dropping. Homer. Boom. I'll wait while you pick it up.

All animals can speak to one another in a kind of grunt, whistle, bark, and squeal, a kind of universal, beasty Esperanto: lion to lamb, bird to dog, moose to cat — except, really, who would ever want to have a lengthy conversation with a cat? Very narcissistic they are. But we, the animal kingdom, ain't got no words or what you would call language. And yes, I know that was bad grammar just then, I was using that for emphasis. I'm not a marsupial. Marsupials are infamous for their inability to understand the rules of grammar (ever try to have a dialogue with a kangaroo? Nearly incomprehensible even if you can penetrate that accent, mate). And who knows what the hell fish are talking about. But I digress. That's very bovine of me. Digression and digestion. It's what we do. We cows have a lot of time on our hooves to chew the cud, as it were. We stand, we eat, we talk, maybe find a salt lick. It's all good.

At least it *was* all good. Till about two years ago. That's when the story I'm telling pretty much begins. My life up until that point was idyllic. I was born on a small farm in upstate New York in the United States. The Bovary clan has been there since time began. My mother and my mother's mother and her mother's mother's mother, etc. The fathers in cow families are pretty much absent. My dad, Ferdinand (I know), used to come around now and then, and I suppose that's how I got all my brothers and sisters. But for the most part, the boys are kept separate from the girls. They like to stare at us from beyond the fence. Sometimes it's a little creepy, to be honest. It's like the boys are a different species, but I don't judge. If I've learned anything in the past two years it's not to judge. I guess what I'm saying is since the beginning of civilization, boys and girls have been kept separate, so we don't expect anything different. It's all I know so I don't stand around wishing my dad were around.

Humans love us. Or I thought so, we all thought so. They love our milk. Now personally, I think it's a little weird to drink another animal's milk. You don't see me walking up to some human lady who just gave birth, saying, "Yo, can I get a taste?" Weird, right? Not gonna happen. It's kinda nasty. But that's why you love us. The ol' milk. Leche. To each his own, I suppose. And every girl grows up knowing that every morning, the farmer is going to come and take our milk. Which is kind of a relief, 'cause we get swollen, and it can feel good to feel all sveltelike and streamlined again after a good milking. Yeah, we care about how we look. And we don't appreciate it that when you people think someone is fat you call them a cow. And pigs aren't very happy about the whole "pig" or "swine" thing, and chickens are pissed too about the "chicken" thing (which secretly makes me happy, 'cause roosters are the biggest pain in the haunches God ever created).

Oh yeah, we believe in God. In the shape of a cow. Not really. Scared you, though, didn't I? But we do believe something made all the somethings in the world — all the animals, animalcules, plants, rocks, and souls. And whether that Maker something is shaped like a cow, a pig, a person, an amoeba, or Jerry Garcia, we don't really know and don't care. We just believe there's a force for life and creation out there. The closest thing people have to it is Mother Earth. But that's just an approximation. And we don't just believe these things, we know them. In our bones and in the bones of our ancestors who lie out there in Old Macdonald's field somewhere.

Man, I am one digressive cow. You're gonna have to get used to it. Homer was pretty digressive too, wasn't he? So I got a precedent there. Before I tell you what happened, let me give you a little more backstory, tell you what my life was like before the Event. That's what I call it — the Event, or the Revelation, or the Day the Patty Hit the Fan. Let me set the scene. Give you some flavor.

Life on a farm. It's pretty chill. Spend a lot of time out in the field hanging with my bffs, getting the hairy eyeball from the bulls. The grass is green on our side, my mom always used to say. She was a great mom, but she disappeared one day, like all cow moms do. We're taught to accept that. That a mom is not forever and it doesn't mean she doesn't love you if she leaves without saying goodbye once the job of raising you from a calf is done. And even though I know this is "the way things are" and "the way things always have been," I still get a little choked up thinking about my mom. She was beautiful — big brown eyes, wicked sense of humor. Never left my side until one day she did. But I'll get to that later. Give me a moment as I think about my mother. Feelings come and go, unless you don't feel them. Then they stay, and hurt, and grow pear-shaped and weird. So when we cows have a feeling, we feel it, till the feeling passes. Then we moo-ve on. Boom. Didn't see that coming, did you?

I recall the days of my childhood through the green grass-colored lens of nostalgia. It all seems so far away and so perfect. Every day a sunny day, even the rainy ones. We had grass and food and a place to sleep and good friends, and always some drama going on with the other animals, but nothing too major. The hierarchy of a farm is very fluid. I don't know if you'd call it a democracy. I think a better term is *live and let live*, unless there are chickens around. Then all bets are off. I don't know if you've read *Animal Farm*. It seems like that's a book all human children have to read. Personally I prefer *Charlotte's Web*, though spiders can be tricky — *Harlot's Web*, anybody? (And eight legs? Really? Two or four is the appropriate number of legs, everybody knows this. Maybe five, maybe. Eight seems indecisive to me, or indulgent; desperate, even. You know?)

Anyway, a normal farm is nothing like the farm in *Animal Farm* — there are no bosses, we're all bosses, and we're what you would call matriarchal, the women run the whole shebang. No matter what the stupid roosters say. We cows have a saying — don't step on my teat and I won't step on yours. And then we add love to that. Animal love. Pure love. Yes, we kill to survive, some of us have to, but it's not the type of killing humans do; there's no hatred or joy, only necessity. We're not Pollyanna. We understand even the fox who steals eggs, and the hawk who snatches away a baby piglet into a horrible death in the sky. It's the way. I

"That's where life happens — out in the field."

thank the grass as I chew it down. You think plants don't have feelings? Maybe not the type of feelings you and I have, but they do have planty feelings, really slow feelings that unfold or blossom over years rather than seconds. To a cow, the world is one big feeling thing.

Here's how it goes:

Monday
SUNRISE: Get milked. You're lucky if you get the middle son or the youngest, the eldest chump is very rough with his hands. He just does not want to be there. I get it, dude, it's way early, but still.

AFTER MILKING: The gates open and out we go into the field, where we'll spend most of the day eating, chewing, talking, gossiping, etc. That's where life happens — out in the field. Sweet green grass and sweeter alfalfa hay.

LATE AFTERNOON: Back into the barn for the night. Another milking and then we usually go to sleep at sundown. We're at one with the rhythms of the earth and whatnot. When my mom was around, she used to tell me stories. I liked the ones where humans act like animals. My mom was a great storyteller, and usually I would fall asleep to the sound of her voice like it was the wind rustling gently through the trees or a brook running over stones.

And then Tuesday, Wednesday, Thursday, Friday, Saturday, and Sunday are exactly the same.

Pretty simple, right? Wake up, milking, eat, day in the field, milking, story, sleep. That was enough for me. I never wanted anything more. I never wanted to live anywhere else. And I wanted the same for my daughters and their daughters forever and always, even though I could never imagine leaving them the way my mother left me. That is, until the Event, the day the earth stood still, the patty-and-fan thing. Then I understood it all, even Mom. And though the knowledge was painful, it led to forgiveness and understanding, and I wouldn't trade that for anything. Innocence is nice, but the world offers us more and it's wrong not to take it. You can't stay a calf forever.

We're almost there. You getting frustrated with all the preamble? The mood lighting? That's the problem with you crazy kids and the video games — no patience. Well, cow time is slow, and I will not be rushed. Gotta go do my job, then a nap, I like me a solid nap. Then the Event.

CHAPTER
TWO

A DAIRY TALE

Okay, I'm back. Let's get into it. Hopefully, I've set the scene for you, the way a farm works in a live-and-let-live manner, the way we understand we're here to provide services to the humans in return for food, shelter, and safety. We didn't ask to come here, right? Did you know that cows are not indigenous to North America? No. My ancestors, my great-great-great-great-great-etc.-grandmother came from somewhere in what humans call the Middle East. That's where the Maker made us and first put our hooves on the ground. They called it the land of milk and honey. And guess who provided the milk? Though I'm told that goats also get milked by humans. Are you kidding me? Come on. No offense, but goat's milk does not compare with cow's milk, unless you're a goat kid. Have you ever seen a cow trying to drink milk from a goat? Case closed.

And now I hear stories of humans milking something called an "almond," and another called a "soy." I've never seen a wild almond or a soy galloping about in its natural habitat, but cow milk is the best. I'd bet three of my four stomachs on it. Of course I'm biased, what else could I be? Bias makes the world go round, sometimes a little too fast. But I digress. And maybe digression isn't really digression, maybe the shortest distance between two mind points is not a straight line. Chew on that.

So there I am, three years old. Mom gone who knows where, but I'm okay. I'm living my life and looking forward to having kids of my own. I'm even looking over the fence at some of those bulls and thinking, "Eh, not so bad." I never thought I'd say that, but that's kind of where I was, and it kind of led me to where I am. So one day, me and my bff Mallory were whispering to each other. Mallory is seriously gorgeous, like she could definitely model. She could be the cow on the milk carton. I'll give you the dialogue, but keep in mind it's not word-for-word, this is an approximation. I'm not a tape recorder. I'm not an elephant. Though I have some friends who are elephants. Super-cool mammals. Good people. Here it is:

MALLORY

I don't know, Elsie, but I kinda wanna go hang out with the bulls all of a sudden. I don't know what's gotten into me.

ELSIE (that's me!)

I know. Me too.

MALLORY

What's wrong with us? When that young bull Frank stomps around and snorts, I get a funny feeling inside and I don't even care that he's got boogers totally all over his nose.

ELSIE

I know, I know. I think my mother told me about this, but only kind of. She said that one day the things that interested me then would be boring, and the things that bored me would be interesting.

MALLORY

Your mom was so cool. Where'd she go?

ELSIE

Yeah. Dunno. Same place as your mom, I guess.

MALLORY

Yeah.

ELSIE

Have you noticed the eldest son sometimes forgets to latch the gate after he milks us? Next time he does it, why don't we just go out and talk to the bulls?

MALLORY

But they'll see us.

ELSIE

We'll do it at night!

MALLORY

You're so smart! The nighttime is the right time. I don't even know where that came from.

ELSIE

Who are you right now?

MALLORY

I do not know! I'm totes cray-cray. Oh, look at what that bull Frank is doing right now. Or is that Steve?

ELSIE

That's Steve.

MALLORY

Yeah, look at him stomp and snort. He is so cool. Good ol' Steve.

ELSIE

I thought you liked Frank.

MALLORY

I do. Frank is the bomb. I kinda like them all.

And then we had a bull session, talked about bulls for about twenty minutes, but I won't tell you what was said 'cause it's private, and I haven't gotten in touch yet with Mallory to make sure she can be a character in my story. My editor says I need clearance. And Mallory is not her real name. It isn't.

And see how that whole scene was kinda written in what's called "screenplay form"? My editor loves that stuff. Big-shot Hollywood producers take note, this practically shoots itself.

So that's what we did. We waited. Seems like we waited forever. The eldest boy, the one with the pimples and the cell phone, all of a sudden got very conscientious about closing the gate, but I knew it wouldn't last. Humans are very easily distracted. Especially by their phones. They have a weird and unnatural attachment to those gadgets. I'm not judging, but it's weird. All right, maybe I am judging. I knew what to do. It was only a matter of time.

CHAPTER
THREE

THE EVENT
(Actually, the Pre-Event)

Sure enough, the time came and I seized it. The eldest was milking me. Roughly, I might add. Look, this isn't a gossipy tell-all; I'm not here to grind axes and settle scores, but sometimes I just gotta calls 'em likes I sees 'em. The brother was rough on the teats. Plus, he's got like the thumb of one hand distractedly on his phone the whole time he's manhandling me. Since then, I have come to learn this is called "texting," and it's a way for people to tell one another stupid things about their day. Oh look, here's a picture of my lunch with an oh-so-witty caption. Oh look, here's a picture of me making a silly face, and another picture of a different face. Selfies, they call 'em, and that makes sense 'cause even though they're sending these pictures to others, it still smells like selfish to me. Is that why they call it an "I phone"? 'Cause it's all about me me me. Like talking to hear yourself talk. Why don't they just communicate in person like normal animals? There's much about people I do not understand.

So there he is, texting away and taking a picture of me and laughing and pressing SEND, and I didn't really appreciate that, so at the perfect moment I just kind of kicked with my right hind leg, not hard to hurt the boy, just hard enough to make him drop his phone.

But first, to set the stage, I had to poop. Pooping while you're getting milked is one of life's great pleasures. You should try it sometime. So I pooped, kicked a little, and he dropped his phone right into what you all call a cow patty. Now I know you think cow patties are gross or a source of humor, but to us, they just are. Another thing about humans I don't quite get is how disgusted they are with poop, even their own. They can't get away from it fast enough, and whenever they step in ours, they curse and try to get it off their boots really fast. Plus, they think poop is totally funny. Like it's the setup of all these jokes they tell one another. I don't get it, man, it's just poop. Poop and farts. What? That make you uncomfortable? That's your problem, Cochise. We all do it. We all do it lots. No big deal. Poopy poop poop fart farty fart fartalicious poopiosity etc. — got it out of your system? And stop blaming me and my gas for global warming. I can't drive a car. Can we move on now?

His phone goes ploop — right into the poop. Ever seen a cow laugh? No, 'cause we do it in private, like Japanese women. I turned away and started laughing, but I kinda faked like I had something in my throat and was coughing. He was pissed! Actually slapped me on the rump. Didn't hurt. You people are small and weak. And then he has to dig his precious phone out of my poop. You think people don't like stepping in poop, man oh man, do they not like getting their hands anywhere near it even more! But he has to. 'Cause it's

15

his phone. If he dropped his phone into a shark's mouth, he'd go in there to retrieve it. Or a volcano. It's like the most important thing in the world.

So his phone is like a quarter of the way in my poop. Standing up straight, like it's surprised to be there. And the boy has to deal with it. He gets down there, and ever so gingerly, like a pimply King Arthur pulling the sword from the stone, he rescues his phone. And then he wipes it on me 'cause he's mad. Like he's punishing me. What do I care? It's my poop. He starts muttering under his breath, grabs the pail of my milk, and stomps out of the barn. And guess what? He forgets to shut the gate. :) Doesn't that mean "smiley face" when you text? Well, here I am, smiling. I wish there were a cow face smiling, but there isn't a way to make it on the keyboard. :(

Yet. :)

CHAPTER
FOUR

THE OPEN GATE

You like that? Chapter titles and whatnot. I've been doing that since the beginning of my story. Fancy, I know, but I want to highlight the concept.

What the open gate means is that, come nightfall, Mallory and I are gonna be able to sneak out and go wherever we want. To the bulls, to the ball game — wherever. The gate opens into a whole new world. Mallory and I are so excited. Especially her. To see Frank, or Steve, or Dino, or whomever. No doubt you've noticed that one of a cow's best features is our long, impossibly thick, luxurious eyelashes. Human women would die for our eyelashes. Come on now, don't be a hater. Every species, like everyone, has a strong point or two. Heavenly eyelashes are one of ours.

Mallory is in her stall applying cow mascara to make her eyelashes even more beautiful, and I suppose make her irresistible to Frank or Steve or whomever it is she thinks she has a crush on. Cow eyeliner is basically some good clean dirt, then you add a touch of water and lay your face down in the mud and then shake your head. If you're lucky more of the dirt will adhere to the lashes and less around your mouth, which is not a good look. Mallory does this and then I do her the solid of

17

licking her face to get the excess dirt. She looks amazeballs. No doubt Frank or Steve is going to find her the most beautiful cow in the world. I'm just excited to get out past the gate. I mean, yeah, I'm kinda into the bulls, but in a way I don't quite get, so I'm a little afraid of it, but really, I'm just looking for adventure. That's the kind of cow I am.

Mallory and I can barely contain our excitement. The day crawls by like a human baby on all fours. It's like the sun decided not to move in the sky; it's just hanging there. It's so hard not to tell anybody about our plans, but we know that if we did that we could ruin it. I notice this one pig looking at me funny, with his head tilted, and a little smile. This pig is named Jerry. So I say, "What, you never saw a cow before?" And I say, "Take a picture, babe, it'll last longer." And he kinda turns away. That's how you handle pigs, gotta be super straightforward 'cause they're really smart at the circuitous-logic-type stuff, too smart for their own good. You gotta psych 'em out. They overthink — so a direct shot will short-circuit them and make them wanna take a nap. Which is what Jerry does. Like I gave him a mental karate-chop sedative. Handled that. I'm like a Jedi sometimes.

Finally, the sun starts to dip beneath our western horizon, maybe my favorite moment of any day. Dusk. Sunset. Love it. Night will not be too far behind, and with night, an adventure, one that will change my life forever.

CHAPTER
FIVE

OUTSIDE THE GATE

See what I did there? I left you on a poetic cliffhanger. And a chapter title again. Gives you a chance to take a break, maybe dog-ear a page, get something to eat, and when you come back, the chapter heading will refocus you on the story. Like a Jedi, I tell you, a Jedi. But really, I'm just thinking about your comfort and enjoyment. :)

It was a pretty moonless night. It was pretty, and it was moonless, so it was pretty moonless. Which was good news for Mallory and me, 'cause it would be harder to see us in the near-total darkness. We waited for what seemed like forever for the rest of the animals in the barn to fall asleep, and for the dogs to stop nosing around. Don't get me wrong, dogs are fine, though about half are bitches, but because they are often allowed to sleep in the house and are considered to be domesticated and man's best friend and all, they tend to have a pretty high opinion of themselves and think whatever they do is the right thing 'cause it's for the boss, the farmer. I actually feel sorry for them a little, 'cause they're neither here nor there, neither fully animal nor fully human; they're caught somewhere between wolf and man, wild and mild, and that must be pretty confusing at times, and sad. Like broccaflower. Dogs are the broccaflower of the animal kingdom.

The two dogs on our farm are called Will and Grace, a couple of border collies. Like I said, smart and stuck-up. So Will and Grace are patrolling around, barking at nothing, saying things to each other like "sector four clear, sector two clear," I mean, come on, it's a farm, dudes, no sectors. Anyway, after they're convinced all the sectors are clear, they run back to the house to go do whatever it is they do in the house. I listen to the sounds in the barn, lots of snoring, some shuffling, but generally the contented, murmurry sounds of sleeping animals. It's a little like music. But this night, I'm not going to stay till the end of the concert. To talk like one of the dogs, I lean over to Mallory and whisper, "It's go-time."

CHAPTER
SIX

GO-TIME

I'd been up to that old gate a thousand times before, but this was different. Everything was different. You know those times in your life that you know are going to change everything? When all your senses are heightened and time seems to stand still and rush ahead all at once? That's how I felt. At the opened gate, to cover my fear, really, 'cause I was so scared I'd already dropped a couple of patties on the walk up, I say to Mallory, to give myself the courage of a joke, "One small step for cow, one giant leap for cowkind . . ." and I nose open the gate. It was that easy. A world changes that easily. With a nudge of a gate, with a step, one step and then you can't go backward, things are never again the same. Ever seen a cow walk backward? Nope. Can't do it, it's not in our nature to go back.

The whole time, Mallory is kinda narrating what we're doing, almost to convince herself that someone else, not her, is doing these things, is sneaking out — "and they're walking up to the gate, and they're pushing the gate open, and, that's right, sports fans, they are walking outside the gate at night — OMG — *they are walking outside the gate at night!*" She's freaking a bit, so I shush her, her eyes are as wide as a deer's, but she's happy, I can tell, she's psyched. She says, "Let's do this." So off we go, step by step, always glancing back at the barn, which all of a sudden seems so small and far away even though we've gone only about ten yards. We also keep an eye on the house to make sure no humans or dogs are alerted.

All quiet. Except in the near distance we could make out a sound, the sound we had come for, the sound we were going toward like Odysseus to the Sirens — the snorting of the bulls.

CHAPTER
SEVEN

BULLS#@T!!!

You like that? My editor told me if I add some sex, curses, and maybe some potty humor, this will sell better to my "audience." I don't know who my audience is. I want everybody to hear this story, but my editor says human adults won't take a talking animal seriously ("Why not?" I asked. "What about *Animal Farm* and *Charlotte's Web*? *Babe*?" And she goes, "Elsie, Elsie, Elsie, times have changed, and anyway, this isn't an allegory, this is a true story . . . blah, blah, blah"). So she's gonna market it as a kids' book, a wolf in sheep's clothing. Which is fine by me, I like kids, but then she says, "Adults are gonna read this book to their kids so you have to sprinkle little inside jokes along the way with some allusions to pop culture from the last thirty years so they don't get too bored. Just make sure you make a reference to *Gilligan's Island* or *Star Wars* or Depeche Mode or Chia Pets or something, cover the decades — sixties, seventies, eighties, nineties, aughts — and the occasional penis joke."

She gave me a bunch of movies to look at to see what she was talking about, but they kinda bored me, to be honest, like they were trying to talk out of both sides of the mouth. But I guess I get what she means. There should be a wink now and then. That's okay. So some of my readers know what's supposed to happen when we get up there with the bulls, you know, cue the funky bass line and the bad acting. That's another thing: humans are so weird about the sex. It's like pooping, folks, everybody does it. That's my next book, *The Educated Flea*. But don't worry. This is a PG story. Wink wink. Hey, man, don't hate the playa, hate the game.

My editor also told me my story should be written "more like a screenplay than a book 'cause that's where the big audience is — not books anymore, but movies." So that's what I've been attempting wherever possible. And she says animated movies are the biggest movies of all, and that animals are often the stars of animated films. I say, "How can I write it like a movie if it's a true story?" And she literally jumps out of her chair and says, "Gold mine! The first animated documentary! Gold mine! Just write out the dialogue without quotes and underneath a character's name and they'll think it's a documentary screenplay *and* it will make it longer to boot. And remember to put something in like 'The names have been changed to protect the blah, blah, blah.'"

We'll see if Hollywood calls. I'll have to lose some weight. I'm as big as a yak. I also have some very specific casting ideas about who should play me, but my editor says if I put them out there, it will step on the toes of the producers. She says producers like to think everything is their idea. So I'll hold my tongue. Jennifer Lawrence.

24

Anyway, I have to admit the sound the bulls were making was a bit mesmerizing. We were drawn to it, Mallory and me, it was like the sweetest music. Sounds that had been stupid to us the day before were now like the Beatles. (Pop culture reference, check.) Weird. I don't get it. But it's natural, happens to us all. We were making our way up to the bulls and the bulls now knew we were heading their way and boy oh boy did they start to get pumped up. Snorting louder and pawing the ground and showing off by running and smashing into one another. Mallory and I were pretty jazzed that they were putting on this whole big show for us. Made us feel like a couple of special cows. Made us feel pretty and . . . bullish. (You're welcome.)

When we got up to the fence, the bulls were like, "Hey there, baby girl . . ." and "Whassup?" trying to be cool, and it was then I realized, yeah, we got outside our gate, but we didn't think about the bulls' gate. Mallory realized this at the exact same moment I did ('cause we're bffs) and we both said, "Oh no! How do we get this gate open?" Now, to be totally honest with you, I was somewhat relieved. I didn't feel I was totally ready to enjoy the company of a bull without a nice, sturdy fence between us, but I couldn't really tell Mallory that. The bulls were freaking me out a little this close up. Weird energy, if ya know what I'm sayin'. The bulls are now like, "You want me to knock down this fence, little lady, 'cause I totally will, I will knock this shit down," and similar-type stuff, and Mallory is just grinning away like a moron. So I say, "Let me go find something I can smash the latch with, something heavy," and Mallory is like a zombie at this point, she's like, "Sure, sure, whatevs," and I'm like, what happened to cows before bulls and hoes before bros? But, really, I get it, I do, and I love her to death, my Mallory girl, wherever you are. So I say I'll be back in a few minutes and I sneak down the hill on little cat's feet.

CHAPTER
EIGHT

OFF THE BEATEN PATH

I don't know what made me head toward the house. I guess it was destiny. Something pulled me toward that house and I followed. I had never been up to the house before in my life. The lights were glowing. It was a dark night, but it was spring and mild. The family had their windows open. I could hear voices coming from within, human voices, but somehow not human voices, very strange. And a flickering light, like a campfire, but not a campfire. I was drawn by the strange voices and the strange, uneven light. I knew it was cray cray, but I had to see what the story was. Curiosity killed the cat, not the cow, so I figured I was safe. I looked back up the hill and I could see the silhouettes of Mallory and the bulls and I could hear them a little, they were laughing and snorting, having a good time, it sounded like. Feeling Mallory was okay up there alone, I crept along the side of the house right up to an open window and looked in.

I didn't know what to make of what I saw. The whole family was in there quietly staring at a lighted box. The people were hushed like the light box was their god and this Box God was talking, or saying words anyway, and the people seemed both transfixed and bored at the same time. The people were eating things out of a bag, crunchy things, and drinking bubbly colored water out of huge cups the size of my snout. These must be part of the Box God's ritual demands, I thought, but I really didn't know what to think. As I said, people are weird. And just as I was about to turn around and leave before I got into trouble, the Box God said something I'll never forget . . .

Cliffhanger!!!

CHAPTER
NINE

THE BOX GOD

This is what I remember the Box God said. It's not perfect, 'cause right after, the world went spinny and warped, and I fainted, but this is what I remember it saying:

"*The small farm is dead, replaced by huge industrial meat farms the size of a small town. Here, at this plant . . .*"

And this is where I stopped hearing, 'cause what I was seeing was so shocking it rocked my world off its axis.

First, I saw chickens in cages, row upon row upon row of cages. The chickens were piled up on one another with barely room to breathe. I'm not a huge fan of chickens, but this was no way to be living. The chickens were hardly able to move, so their talons actually grew around the wire of the cages and the humans sometimes had to cut their feet off to remove them. I started to cry big wet tears, which made what I was looking at blurry and kaleidoscopic, even more surreal. Then they showed pigs, hundreds upon hundreds of them all penned in together too. That didn't seem too bad, pigs like to hang with their own, but still, it was way crowded and filthy and sad.

"And then they showed the cows."

And then they showed the cows.

The cows were being kept in this huge building, separated from one another by these tight metal chutes. But that's not what was bad. Because the merciless Box God showed what happened to the cows next: a man held a metal rod up to the cow's head, and the cow's legs just gave way like that, and she collapsed, dead. Murdered. One after another, snuffing out life as if it were just flipping a light switch from on to off.

And then the Box God showed the lifeless carcasses of cows being hung up on big metal hooks and cut up, stripped of skin and dismembered like in a horror movie, blood everywhere, all I remember is blood. A faceless man with a hose rinsing a room of blood. And then some discussion of veal that I cannot to this day think about without throwing up and changing the subject, and I can only refer to as the "V." Or the "V word." And the blood. Rivers of blood. Oceans of blood. A world of blood. The blood of my kind. I emptied the contents of all four of my stomachs. And then I passed out.

CHAPTER
TEN

I AWAKE

I don't know how long I was out. It couldn't have been that long, because the Box God was still talking about "meat," which by now I know is animal flesh — cows, pigs, chickens, turkeys, dogs in some countries (hey, if you're gonna eat me, why not eat a dog?), monkeys, deer, bear, ostrich, ants — you get the picture. The list goes on and on. Humans will eat almost anything if you put a little salt and butter on it. And the butter is made from our milk. Makes me feel oddly complicit and guilty.

As I was coming to, I noticed everything had changed. Yes, it all looked the same — even though now the clouds had cleared and the moon glowed like a new quarter in the heavens, but for the first time, I could make out a face in the moon, the so-called man in the moon, and his mouth was open and his eyes were wide in horror and disbelief. I could smell the grass, which had always been such a comfort to me and reminded me of my mother, but there was a sour taste in my mouth, like bile, that was ruining any scent. I did not like the world and wanted only blackness and silence. I wanted to get away from these humans and their Box God and their endless consumption of things.

On unsteady legs, I started back up the hill to the barn. I don't know how long I'd been gone — an hour, three hours, five minutes, a lifetime? — but when I got back, all the animals were still asleep. Except for Mallory, who was standing there with a huge smile on her face.

CHAPTER
ELEVEN

THE BIRDS AND THE BEES
(in screenplay form)

MALLORY

OMG!!! OMG!!! OMG!!! OMG!!!

(There were about three hundred more OMGs, but I don't want you to think I'm padding my story.)

ELSIE

What? What? Take a chill pill, girlfriend.

MALLORY

Nothing will ever be the same again!

ELSIE

You can say that again.

MALLORY

No way! Did you hook up?

ELSIE

Hook up? Me? No, no, go on, tell me what happened.

(I didn't really want to hear, but I couldn't really tell MALLORY what had happened down at the house with the people and the Box God. Not yet. I still was processing it myself. It was like a bad dream that was not quite over.)

MALLORY

It was full-on *West Side Story*. Frank goes to Steve and he's like, "Yo, dude, she's a black-and-white Holstein like me, my mother was a black and white, so she's my girlfriend," and Steve was like, "Yeah, if it was the fifties maybe, but it's not like that anymore and red bulls can be with anyone, anyone can be with anyone." And I thought, Yeah, you go, Steve, yeah, that makes total sense. They were totally fighting over me. Elsie? Earth to Elsie?

ELSIE

Yeah, yeah, they were totally fighting over you.

(I was trying to listen, but I was totally zoning in and out. I couldn't erase the images of cows hung on hooks, bleeding, bleeding . . . Stop! I told my mind, but I couldn't. Like when my mother always used to say, "Don't think about pink cows," and then of course pink cows is all you can think about. But these cows weren't pink, they were red and bleeding, bleeding . . . Stop!)

MALLORY

They woulda fought over you too, mamacita, but you disappeared. Where'd you go?

ELSIE

Nowhere. Okay, so they're getting all Jets and Sharks with you. What's with you? You look different. Your mascara is running.

MALLORY

I am different. You look different too.

ELSIE

I am different. Go on. So tell me. I hang upon your every word.

MALLORY

So Steve and Frank and these other guys — I think there were like four or five, um, Jimmy C., Matty, and Jose maybe was it? And . . .

ELSIE

Names not important, cut to the chase.

MALLORY

How did you know there was a chase?

ELSIE

It's an expression . . .

MALLORY

Okay, so they do this thing where they're gonna fight, and they snort and stomp and make weird noises, and then they do fight! It was a real fight! They were fighting over me, but I could tell they weren't really trying to hurt one another, that it was more of a show. A delicious exhibition of bullness.

ELSIE

The chase?

MALLORY

Oh yeah, okay, the chase . . . so they ram into one another a few times and chase one another around, but then Frank kinda gives up and says something like, "You can have her, she's not so pretty anyway . . ."

ELSIE

That's hurtful. What a dickhead.

MALLORY

Whatever. He's a loser.

ELSIE

I thought you liked Frank.

MALLORY

Liked, duh. Past tense, as in, no more, bae, I am moving on.

ELSIE

So the other guys take off and you're left there alone with Frank.

MALLORY

Steve.

ELSIE

Steve. Sorry.

MALLORY

So we're hanging out there, by the fence, and he's all kinda out of breath from the half-fake fighting, and I can see his breath, and I can smell it.

ELSIE

Ew.

MALLORY

Not ew. I liked it. And he's like all cool now, he's like, "Babe, I can eat this much grass," and "Babe, I could escape this place anytime, I just choose to stay 'cause it's a cush gig . . ." and on and on.

ELSIE

Right.

MALLORY

So then he presses his lips up against the fence.

ELSIE

Get out.

MALLORY

Yes, ma'am, and he closes his eyes, and just stays there like a statue, so I kissed him . . .

ELSIE

No way!

MALLORY

Way!

ELSIE

Shut the front door! Was it all gross and slobbery?

MALLORY

No, it was, it was . . . I can't describe it . . . you would think that exchanging fluids from your mouth with a guy would be the grossest thing in the world, but it wasn't gross. It was rad. I'm in love.

ELSIE

You're not in love. You barely know him.

MALLORY

That's what love is, Elsie, when you're crazy about someone you don't really know. I'm gonna make calves with him.

I was gonna argue with Mallory, talk some sense into her, but I could tell she was beyond reason at this point, that just as everything — the moon, the grass, the breeze — reminded me of the red death right now, everything reminded her of Steve. And of love. And I thought about telling her what I'd seen, and then I thought, who am I to rain on her parade? I looked over at her and she was lit up like a June night filled with fireflies, and for a brief moment I forgot about what had happened to me, and I was happy. Happy for Mallory, happy for Steve, happy for the world. Happy. And I closed my eyes and slept.

CHAPTER
TWELVE

UNCOMFORTABLY NUMB
(*see* Floyd, Pink)

When I awoke, the middle child was milking me. I must have been awake before that, but I was kind of sleepwalking, half of me could not stop thinking of what I'd seen, which left only half of me to be awake and conscious and make my way through my day. I had always liked the middle child, he was gentle, and he liked to talk to me while he milked me, to tell me about his problems, problems at school, with his parents, with his obnoxious older brother. I guess he thought I was safe, that I didn't understand a word he said. I was always there for him. But not today. Today, I did not like people. None of them. And I guess it was affecting my milk, 'cause the boy kept asking me, "What's wrong, girl?" and taking my face in his hands, and looking deep into my eyes, and petting the top of my head, which I had always loved, but today I just wanted to spit at him or ram him. So that's what I did. I clocked him one right on the chin with my forehead and sent both him and the milk pail tumbling over.

I recognized the look in the boy's eyes now. I recognized it because I could feel it on my own face. It was like looking in a mirror. It was the look of betrayal, of being betrayed. And we just stood there frozen for a moment, me and the boy, staring at each other with our betrayed faces. I could see a tear forming in his eye, and for a moment, I almost felt bad. Almost. But then that almost feeling went away, and I realized I couldn't feel anything anymore. That I would never feel anything again. Ever. I felt dead inside. I was completely numb. I lowered my head and charged him again.

CHAPTER
THIRTEEN

THE BLACK DOG

I guess the middle boy was embarrassed at getting pushed around by a cow and didn't tell anybody, 'cause there were no repercussions from the head-butting incident. The ensuing months were kind of a blur to me. It could have been a week, a year, ten years. The thing is I didn't care. I think humans refer to this state of depression as the "black dog" and I don't really know why that makes sense, but there you have it — I had the black dog, and he was at my side morning, noon, and night, like he was my friend, but I knew he wasn't.

My mind would just turn over and over constantly like an old vinyl record stuck in a groove.

(Hi, parents! You can take a moment to explain to your child what vinyl is, or what a record player is, or what music is, for that matter; you can even tell them about the Led Zeppelin song "Black Dog" if you want to bore the crap out of them. They don't care about your music. They think it's lame. But tell them something to make them understand the mental state that approximates the skipping back and forth in a groove on vinyl.)

It was like I was banging my head against a wall trying to kill the pain or trying to break through the wall, or both.

And in fact, I was banging my head against the side of the barn quite regularly. So much so that Mallory took me aside one day and said she was concerned about me, that I was rubbing the fur off my forehead and if I made myself bald no bull would want me. As if I cared. And then Mallory told me she was pregnant. That she was carrying Steve's calf. And I was happy for her, but I knew that was no longer a life that I wanted. I didn't want to bring another cow into this awful world. I didn't tell her that, though. I kissed her pretty snout and said I was happy for her, and I leaned into her and closed my eyes, and when I opened them, there he was again, standing right beside me with a tennis ball in his mouth, waiting: the black dog.

CHAPTER
FOURTEEN

MOM

Banging your head over and over against a wall is not as bad as it sounds. Or rocking back and forth, or pacing like a panther in a zoo. It's like you're going over the same ground again and again and again, knowing that you will eventually wear a path so deep that you will break through to the knowledge that you seek, break out of this world that makes you want to bang your head against a wall and into another, better one.

So that's what happened. One day, as I was banging my head against the stall wall, I stopped and just spoke one word: *Mom*. I just kept repeating that word over and over, *Mom, Mom, Mom*. And I realized I'd been heartbroken over her disappearance, always nodding when people told me that's what happened on a farm, that the moms and dads leave when the babies are ready to be moms and dads, but inside, I always heard a voice asking, Why did you leave me? Why did you leave me, Mom?

I stopped banging my head because I realized Mom didn't leave me. She was taken away. She was taken away and killed, and then she was eaten. I felt the bile rising again in me from stomachs three and four, and I vomited all over the ground, and maybe I passed out. It was horrible, but it was also freeing. I realized I'd been angry at my mom for leaving and now I wasn't angry anymore. All my anger was now trained on the humans who had betrayed me, and betrayed her even worse.

You humans drink our milk and eat the eggs of the chickens and the ducks. Isn't that enough for you? Isn't it enough that we give you our children and what's meant for our children? And if not, when is it enough? All you humans do is take, take, take from the earth and its beautiful creatures, and what do you give back? Nothing. I know humans consider it a grave insult to be called an animal. Well, I would never give a human the fine distinction of being called an animal, because an animal may kill to live but an animal never lives to kill. Humans have to earn the right to be called animals again.

CHAPTER
FIFTEEN

AN APOLOGY

I apologize because I want this book to be fun and not preachy, and I argued with my editor 'cause I wanted to leave some of the more incendiary, direct-address, polemical stuff in. My editor says, "You do realize you are insulting your entire audience, i.e., the human race? Not what I'd call a winning strategy. Cows don't buy books."

And I say, "I know, but sometimes you just gotta speak your mind."

And my editor argues, "But they've heard it all before, this is not the original part of your story."

So I say, "I don't care if they have to hear it a thousand times more, maybe it's like banging their heads against a wall, maybe this is me banging their heads against a wall and one day the wall will break or their heads will break and they will get it." And my editor says, "They get it, they just don't care."

"Then they just get it with their minds, intellectually, because if they got it with their hearts and souls, they would change, they would change and rejoin the animal kingdom and once again be proud to be called animals. Until that day, I will keep banging their tiny heads against a wall. You can't just wear the food chain around your neck like a bauble or necklace. You're part of it and if you keep treating it with disdain, that chain will strangle you. Do you know how much I am leaving out in the service of being 'entertaining'? Do you know that the alfalfa they like to feed us (and I am a freak for the 'falfa — guilty) takes so much water to grow that it is leading to water shortages? An unnatural chain is being forged. Do you know that the rampant use of antibiotics on livestock — which cuts down on bacterial diseases that would decimate pigs, chickens, and cows forced into unimaginably cramped living conditions, thereby making that obscene overcrowding possible — is also enabling diseases to mutate and adapt resistance to these self same antibiotics? That much of these antibiotics enter the soil and water table through our poop, and we are seeing an appearance of Frankensteinian superbugs and a return of diseases that had been made practically extinct by the medical advances of the previous century? Everything is connected. Everything. That breeze you just felt is a butterfly fluttering his wings in Thailand. Do you want me to go on? I have a list here as long as a giraffe's neck."

"Oh God, no, my eyes are glazing over." My editor yawns. "You're banging my head against the wall right now. Nobody wants to read that crap. People like to be made to feel a lighter shade of guilty, not terrified and shamed. But go ahead, keep it in, shoot yourself in the foot."

So I say, "I can't shoot myself in the foot." And she asks, "Why not?" And I say, "No hands!"

And we laugh.

And she says, "A spoonful of sugar helps the globe-warming, drought-inducing, superresistant-bacteria-creating medicine go down. Don't forget the spoonful of sugar, sugar. We can also recommend to parents that reading this particular chapter to their children guarantees they will fall asleep immediately."

I apologize, but I was an angry young cow at that point in my life, and fully taken with making stands against the Man. I refused to be called Elsie anymore 'cause that was what humans liked to call all cows, and I told all the other animals to call me "Elsie Q" because I didn't know my real name, the Q standing for question mark. Clever, right? And I even had my own ready-made theme song by substituting Elsie Q for Suzy Q. I like the way you walk, I like the way you moo, Elsie Q.

And I guess the force of this revelation about my mom was too much for me and I passed out. Again. 'Cause when I woke up, Jerry the pig was eating my vomit. Don't say "Gross," don't judge. We animals don't waste anything. If one man's trash is another man's treasure, well, one cow's vomit is another pig's dinner. And I looked at him and smiled because I loved my mom again and I was free and he looked at me and smiled and said, "Deeeee-licious!"

CHAPTER
SIXTEEN

FREEISH BIRD
(*see* Skynyrd, Lynyrd)

So I was free. Ish. Yes, I was still stuck on the farm, but I was free inside, in my mind, which is the true place of freedom. I got into the habit of opening the gate at night, and with my mind-freedom came a new way of looking at things, and I looked at the latch, and it was simple to open with my tongue. Things that used to mystify me were so simple now.

And I would just open the latch at night after everyone was asleep and go wandering, usually up in the hills. Away from the bulls. I didn't care about boys.

As I'd wander, my mind would kind of turn off and I'd go into this meditative state where I could talk to my mother. And we would have the most amazing conversations. Some were replays of old talks we'd actually had when she was with me, and some were new ones that would just come to me. Before you knew it, I would hear those stupid roosters start to crow and it would be morning. I was free, yes, but I was still sad somewhere deep inside.

One night, as I wandered through the hills, chatting in my mind with my mom over some insignificant thing like how many times you chew cud before you swallow it, she said to me, "Maybe you should go back down to the house." I said, "I'm never going down there again, I hate people." And she said, "Don't hate. Hate is like a poison you make for your enemy that you end up swallowing yourself." And I said, "Nice one, Obovine-Wan Kenobi." And she said, "Why don't you walk down there, maybe you didn't get the whole story, maybe there's more to learn from the Box God." I said, "As if." And she answered, "Elsie, do you know how proud of you I am? Do you know? Do you know I love you to the nth degree? Do you know how beautiful you are and smart and how I think about you every day and love you and no matter how long my life was, it was a good life because I had you?"

And I started to cry, again. Okay, I'm the town cryer. Guilty. I've never understood how love can hurt so much, but I guess it's a different hurt from anything else. Not like a cracked hoof, more like a bear hug of the heart. But then I found myself all the way down the hill, by the side of the house.

CHAPTER
SEVENTEEN

A WHOLE NEW WORLD
(see Aladdin)

The Box God was talking to the people. I could tell because of their obedient quiet and the flickering of the light. If you people think lambs are silent, check yourselves out while you're praying to the Box God — passive and drooling. So I knew I was pretty safe looking through the window, because the humans were zoned out in a trance, like a night of the living dead. They were all watching something called the Discovery Channel. I know this because they broke out of their stupor long enough to fight over "channels." I realized that the Box God is not just one god, but many gods in one box, and with a magic plastic wand, humans can switch from god to god at any given moment.

It seemed that everyone in the family wanted to worship different gods. The youngest girl wanted to worship the Nickelodeon God, the dad wanted to worship the ESPN God, the oldest, obnoxious son wanted to worship a goddess named Playboy or the Showtime God, while the mom was happy with this Discovery God. Mom won out. Everybody else except the mom and the young girl left the room grumbling, and then I realized that all humans must have a Box God in their own rooms, because the flickering lights started emanating from windows in bedrooms all over the house. What a strange god that instead of bringing people together, divides them.

So I'm kind of enjoying the Discovery God 'cause there are lots of pretty pictures of faraway lands. And it mentions that the name of this one place is India, and that seems to me a beautiful word, and then there are pictures of poverty and people suffering, but there are also cows in a lot of the pictures and I get that feeling of dread that the god is going to start showing these cows getting slaughtered and eaten again, but instead the god says that cows are "sacred" in India, which means respected and special, and he shows pictures of people being really nice to cows and even putting jewelry on them and making them look exotic and pretty. The god says that cows are considered gods themselves in this India place and that no one eats them.

Then the older, obnoxious son runs into the room, grabs the magic wand, and switches the channel to a bunch of men in uniform hitting and chasing and trying to catch a ball. And I learn that the ball is made of the hide of dead horses (cowhide since '74 — that awful summer) and each time the ball gets the slightest bit dirty, they throw it out like it's no good, like there's an inexhaustible supply of horses to kill to make more balls, and for all I know there is. And the thing the men wear to cushion their soft little human hands from the hard ball is called a "glove" and is made of something called "leather," which is just a polite way of saying "the skin of dead cows." And right before I pass out I think: Is there no end to your cruelty?

CHAPTER
EIGHTEEN

INDIA

Over and over in my mind, I turn the word over and over: *India*. India. Like a jewel you might turn in your pocket. India India. I grew distant with this knowledge, distant from the other animals. I became fixated on the house and more secrets I might learn inside it. I learned what signs to look for when the family was going to be away for a while — the suitcases stacked in the car, etc. — and then I would go down to the house and continue my research. I found out so many things. I found children's books where animals were beloved and even heroes. Even cows. Cows were heroic to the children in these books. A cow even jumped over the moon in one. Admittedly, it got unbelievable by the end and totally lost me when the dish ran away with the spoon (I mean, come on), but still, that was one bad cow.

I was confused at how people could mistreat and eat us on the one hand and then celebrate us on the other for qualities they admired. It was then I realized that humans were very complicated and confused and I could spend the rest of my life puzzling them out. I decided I didn't have time to do that. I would spend the few years I had left on this planet trying to figure myself out, trying to figure out the mind of the cow, and if there was any time left over, then maybe, maybe, I'd think about humans again.

I found other books with maps and charts that showed every part of the world, showed me where this magical land of India was. It truly existed, this place where the people had wised up and realized that we cows were gods too. There were so many other lands and countries, more than I could memorize. I thought about how lucky those cows were that were born in India and got to spend their lives there. And then I thought: Why not me? I thought: ***WHY CAN'T I GO TO INDIA?***

CHAPTER
NINETEEN

OPERATION INDIA

I became obsessed. All day long, 24/7, I thought of India and little else. I grew apart from Mallory, who was swelling bigger every day, and that made me sad, but I was now a cow on a mission. I thought constantly about how I might get there. I knew it was far, far away, on the other side of the world actually, and that I would have to cross an ocean. (Ever seen a cow swim? Exactly.) And I wasn't one of those cows who could just jump over the moon to get there. No, I had to get on a plane. Where would I find a plane? In a city. Where was the nearest city? About fifty miles away, within walking distance. So if I could make it to a city, I could make it to an airport, and if I could make it to an airport, I could find a plane going to India, and if I could find a plane going to India, I could get on it. It was a plan. Yes, there were a lot of ifs in it, but it wasn't impossible. And it was so much better than the alternative: death, being eaten and turned into shoes, jackets, couches, car interiors, and baseball gloves.

So I committed myself to it. Operation India. I was going to wait till the end of winter, when the walking weather would be better, and then I was going to walk to the city and get on a plane. I started to believe.

But I also started to feel guilty. I would be leaving Mallory and my other cow friends and cow workers behind. Even those stupid bulls didn't deserve their fate, same with the stupid chickens, and the pigs and horses. Keeping the knowledge to myself started to eat away at me, so I decided I had to tell someone about my plan: Mallory.

One night, when everyone was asleep again, I nudged her with my snout . . .

ELSIE

Mallory, Mals — wake up . . .

MALLORY

Ugh, I feel like such a fat cow . . . What is it?

ELSIE

I need to tell you something.

MALLORY

What? Why you've been such a bitch lately, is that what you're gonna tell me?

ELSIE

Well, yeah . . . yeah. And also . . .

And then I told her pretty much everything I told you, pretty much the way I told it to you.

In the movie version, you'd have cool music playing, preferably a big hit from last summer, as I talk animatedly to Mallory and you see her wide eyes go even wider. Kind of a montage but not totally. Look, I'm not telling the director what to do, I am merely suggesting.

(But that would be the best way to shoot it, that's all I'm gonna say.)

When I finished, Mallory's mouth was wide open and I could've tipped her over very easily, she was that stunned. And by the way, cow tipping is stupid and we're onto it. Maybe we'll start some human tipping, or maybe we just feel like lying down and sleeping and don't mind getting pushed over by the likes of you — ever think of that, genius? You know who you are.

MALLORY

OMG.

ELSIE

I know, right.

MALLORY

No way.

ELSIE

Yes way, and I am going to —

MALLORY

Shut the —

58

ELSIE

Overlapping

Shut the front door.

MALLORY

— front door.

There was a long silence between us. Reminded me of the old times when we were so close we didn't even have to speak to know what the other was thinking. Sistas. Then . . .

MALLORY

What are you gonna . . .

ELSIE

Operation India.

MALLORY

Catchy.

ELSIE

Thank you.

MALLORY

You gotta.

ELSIE

Gotta what?

Go.

Like I said — Mals and me: sistas.

CHAPTER
TWENTY

BABE, I'M GONNA LEAVE YOU
(*see* **Zeppelin, Led**)

It took weeks for Operation India to come into crystal-clear focus. I had maps I had to deal with and figuring out the best way to get into the city without somebody reporting a lost cow. Once I got there, I had no idea how I was going to get on a plane, I just knew I couldn't wait any longer. As I was sleeping one night deep in conversation with my mother, I felt something rooting around my feet. I nearly jumped out of my skin when I saw it was Jerry the pig. He had curlicues made of weeds dangling from his ears and he was carrying an old, tattered, leatherbound book that he held with great reverence. I believe in the screenplay this is called the beginning of Act Two:

JERRY

'Sup?

ELSIE

'Sup, yourself.

JERRY

I mean what is up? What is up with you? What is afoot? What's with all the maps and the whispering with Mallory at night?

ELSIE

Nothing.

JERRY

I'll tell you what I think is up. I think you're planning to get outta Dodge.

ELSIE

As if.

JERRY

Don't stonewall me, cow. You're thinking of makin' a break, skedaddling, blowing this Popsicle stand, makin' like a banana and splitting, makin' like a tree and leavin' on a jet plane, bustin' a moooo-ve . . .

(Here's the thing about JERRY — he won't stop saying these obsessive strings of synonymous figures of speech till you stop him, it could literally go on forever. So to maintain my own sanity, I had to stop him.)

ELSIE

Okay. So what if you're right, so what if I am?

62

JERRY

Well, did you ever stop to think of what will happen to the rest of us if you vamoose, if you fly
the coop, if you go all goodbye yellow brick
road —

ELSIE

You'll be fine.

JERRY

No, we won't. The farmer will come down on us like
a ton of bricks, like the hand of God, like —

ELSIE

Okay. What's your point? Why is that my problem?

JERRY

My point is, I wanna go too.

ELSIE

No. No way.

JERRY

You think you're the only one who knows the lay of
the land? You think you're the only one who knows
which way is up, which side your bread is buttered
on —

ELSIE

Jerry!

JERRY

Sorry — that's like a thing with me, I know. I'll keep
an eye on it, you know, note-to-self it, stick a pin in
it, damn, sorry — what I'm sayin' is I know where
the truffles are, woman. They're gonna eat me just
like they're gonna eat you. It's a damn holocaust in
here.

(I fell silent. I knew JERRY was right, but I didn't
know what I could do. A cow traveling is bad enough,
but a cow and a pig, fugeddaboutit. JERRY kept on,
though.)

JERRY

And I got skills. I got mad skills. I got skills to pay
the bills. Pigs are wicked smart. We are well liked. I
can help.

ELSIE

Look, Jerry, even if I could take you, the same thing
is going to happen to you in India. They'd eat you
there as soon as they'd look at you. Apparently pork
is quite tasty.

JERRY

Low blow, dude. Can you say "hamburger"?

ELSIE

I'm sorry. But it's true. Cows are sacred in India, but
pigs are just, well, pigs.

JERRY

You got your map there?

(And I did. I had stolen a map of the world and a couple of *Encyclopaedia Britannica* volumes from the house to research and figure out all my routes. I knew the family wouldn't notice their absence, 'cause they now got all their information from their phones. Come to think of it, a phone would be handy, but how could I ever work the touch screen with my big ol' hooves?)

JERRY

Hoof it over.

Jerry unrolled the map with his mouth, getting pig mucus all over it, which I did not appreciate.

JERRY

Looky here.

He pointed with his flat, circular snout to somewhere in the Middle East, the original place that cows come from, pretty far away from glorious India.

ELSIE

So? Iraq?

JERRY

No, not Iraq. Here, right over here. Israel, baby.

ELSIE

Israel? What's in Israel?

JERRY

It's nothing in Israel. It's what they do in Israel, or more precisely what they don't do.

ELSIE

What, Jerry, what do they do or not do in Israel?

JERRY

It's a little thing I like to call "kosher."

ELSIE

What's kosher?

JERRY

It's an ancient dietary regimen of the Jews. Prohibitions. Commandments. Restricti-on-ays. [*He said it like it was a Spanish word.*]

ELSIE

What are Jews?

JERRY

It's a long story, some say the greatest story ever told, but basically, Jews are Christians with longer sideburns. And a better sense of humor.

ELSIE

Wha?

66

JERRY

And funny hats.

ELSIE

Wha?

JERRY

The yarmulke . . . the original Hair Club for Men.

ELSIE

Wha?

JERRY

You with all the wha, wha, wha . . . keep your eye on the ball, cow, keep your eye on the doughnut and not the hole, and pick up what I am layin' down. The ancient Jews thought pigs were unclean for some reason that historians argue about, they called us swine, they called us "traif" (along with shellfish, don't ask). They were disgusted by us. Can you imagine? I cannot. [*He held up the old book.*] These are the people of the book. The word, the law.

ELSIE

What book word law?

JERRY

This is the Torah, in the Old Testament, but I just call it the testament 'cause it didn't need a new one, got everything right the first time around.

"Call me Shalom."

ELSIE

Fine, fine, but what you describe sounds terrible, why would you wanna go somewhere you're hated?

JERRY

Hatred can be as useful as love.

ELSIE

You lost me, bro.

JERRY

Because they hate us pigs so much they won't eat us!

ELSIE

Ahhhhh . . .

JERRY

It'll be heaven. I'll walk down the street, and people will get outta my way like I'm Clint Eastwood. Nobody will talk to me, they won't even look at me, but best of all, I won't wind up on their damn plates next to some friggin' apple sauce!

I had to admit, Jerry had a point, a very valid point, and I agreed that being a pariah was better than being eaten, especially for someone with the stunted social skills of a Jerry, who might actually enjoy living the life of an antagonist. I'd be a god and he'd be a devil, and we both would live. Humans are ridiculous, but we were desperate. So I relented. I nodded. I said that he could come and I would do my best to get me to India

69

and him to Israel, but I couldn't promise anything. He smiled, grunted, kissed my knee with his snout, and said — "Next year in Jerusalem, my friend."

Then he added, "Call me Shalom."

CHAPTER
TWENTY-ONE

LET'S GO: TURKEY

Finally I had my route to the city plotted out. Jerry, I mean Shalom, was a pain in the tuchus, but he was proving to be pretty helpful with logistics. I have to admit, Shalom is pretty smart. One night, about three days before Jerry and I were gonna make a break for it, I was just standing, thinking about life in India and how much fun it would be to be worshipped as a god, when I heard a very strange noise by the barn door, a kind of shuffling and a gargling sound, like somebody was simultaneously trying to swallow a bunch of marbles while saying the word *marble*. Certain sections of the barn were lit where the windows let the moon in, and whatever it was was walking, or maybe *strutting* is a better word, to a spot on the ground where I could see who it was. A turkey.

Now, we cows don't know the turkeys well at all. They are kind of kept in an area away from us. Sometimes we pass them on the way out to pasture, but we rarely talk. They've always struck me as really nervous, the kind of nervous that wears out your sympathy and just ends up making you nervous too, so you avoid it, and them. But I couldn't avoid this turkey 'cause he was walking right at me.

TURKEY

Are you Q, the cow formerly known as Elsie Bovary?

ELSIE

Who wants to know?

TURKEY

The name is Turkey, Tom Turkey.

Now, he said this the way "Bond, James Bond" says it, so I really had to stifle a laugh. I acted like I had a chicken feather in my throat.

TOM

Meleagris gallopavo, Mama-san. Not to be confused with *Numida meleagris,* the helmeted guinea fowl. You okay there, little lady? 'Cause I totally know the Heimlich maneuver.

ELSIE

No, no, I'm good, I'm good.

(As he got closer, I could tell this turkey didn't take care of himself. He was rail-thin and his feathers were all uncombed, flying off in every direction. Even so, he seemed a bit vain and impressed with himself, and walked with the confident strut of a pimp from a '70s blaxploitation movie.)

TOM

I guess right about now, you're asking yourself, "Self, what is that gorgeous hunk of turkey man all about and why is he pimp-rollin' my lucky way?"

ELSIE

No. Not even close.

TOM

C'mon, baby, let's be real.

ELSIE

I was wondering when was the last time that little flightless bird had a meal. Boy oh boy, you are thin.

TOM

Thank you for noticing.

ELSIE

I've got some slop here the pigs left and some chicken feed the chickens didn't finish.

And with that, the natural nerves of the turkey overwhelmed him, and he lost all semblance of pimp-roll bravado, reacting to the food the way Dracula does to a cross.

TOM

Keep that food away from me! Are you insane?

ELSIE

What? You just looked like you could use a meal, is all. You look terrible.

TOM

I'm all muscle, baby girl. All muscle, gristle, and bone.

TOM *struck a muscleman pose, the "archer."*

ELSIE

You should eat. And don't call me "baby girl."

TOM

I can't eat.

ELSIE

Why not?

TOM

'Cause I'll get fat.

ELSIE

Oh, you're one of those anorexics! I've heard about that. Or bulimic. Or body dysmorphic disorder. Are you a duck trapped in a chicken trapped in a turkey's body? A turducken? Which is it now?

TOM

None of that! I'm totally compos mentis in the *cabeza*. You got it all wrong; I'm not a jive turkey. November is just a few months away!

74

ELSIE

And what happens in November, you fly south and wanna look good in your mankini? Oh wait, you can't fly . . .

TOM

Do I have to spell it out for you? The fourth Thursday of every November — Thanksgiving!!! Everyone in America, we are talking millions of people, will eat a turkey. Millions of us get slaughtered every year on one black day!!!

ELSIE

That sucks, but at least it's only one day.

TOM

That's why I'm all skinny. I'm hoping they'll look at me and think, "That ain't no drumstick."

ELSIE

Good plan. Good luck with that.

TOM

I need more than luck. And I have an actual plan.

ELSIE

Oh geez . . . here we go . . .

TOM

I hear you have a map.

You try keeping a secret on a farm. Impossible. They don't say "gossiping like hens" for nothing. I shoved the map over to the bird. He unrolled it with his beak. I was impressed with his dexterity.

TOM

Right here.

I looked where he was beaking — seemed like around the Middle East again. Seemed like everything always led back to the Middle East.

ELSIE

Iraq?

TOM

Not Iraq. Turkey!!!

ELSIE

Yes, that's right, Turkey is the name of a country.

TOM

Yes, and do you think for a moment that they are going to eat the thing their country is named after? That's my country, those are my peeps. I'll be like royalty over there — instead of being on a hero, I will be a hero! They may make me king. My name is on all the money. I'll be rich as Croesus. I gotta get to Turkey!! And, just as an aside, however we get there, can we not go through that country called Hungary? It sounds like a nightmare for all of us. Just the name makes me shiver: *Hungary*. And all the scary, hungry Hungaryarians that live there.

ELSIE

Okay, I concede you have a point, Turkey, but I'm already traveling heavy with a pig at my side that I gotta get to Israel. A bird is just gonna slow me down even more, and what's more, you're a flightless bird. You're a bird that can't fly. You're an oxymoron.

TOM

Hurtful. Calling me a moron.

ELSIE

I said "oxymoron."

TOM

Any kind of moron. Just hurtful.

ELSIE

I got no time for niceties.

TOM

Okay, but what if I added value to the enterprise, rather than subtracted? Because that's what I'm all about — being additive, not subtractatative . . .

ELSIE

What are you getting at?

*And I didn't know where he pulled it out from,
'cause turkeys don't have any pockets, but in the
slivered moonlight, he was pushing toward me what
was clearly a cellular phone, exactly the thing I'd been
coveting for the journey.*

ELSIE
Impressive. But it's of no use to me. I can't work it
with these hooves and neither can Jerry, er, Shalom.

TOM
Check it.

*I swear that cheeky turkey was winking at me. And
with that, he began pecking at the phone like a high
school girl at 3:01. He had the weather, he had
On-Star, Uber, even Siri was at his whim. I swal-
lowed a gasp, tried to cover my glee, and said —*

ELSIE
You're in.

CHAPTER
TWENTY-TWO

A MOMENT

The next couple of days passed in a blur. The nights were filled with hushed planning as Shalom, Tom, and I finalized our route, and tried to figure out the best use of the phone without running the battery out. We also had to practice walking on two legs, at least Shalom and I did, so we could better fit in without drawing so much attention to ourselves as four-legged creatures, and that didn't come so easy. We worked our tails off at it night after night.

Think of this (screenplay alert!) like the "Feeling Strong Now" montage from *Rocky*, where he's training for the big fight. Almost exactly like that, except it doesn't end with someone punching the hanging carcass of a cow. (Does that sound bitter? Maybe I am a little. I'll have to think about that.)

The afternoon before the night we were to leave, all of us cows were out to pasture. Mallory was huge now. She was ready to give birth at any moment, and I was sorry I might not be there for that, when lo and behold, she gave out a low grunty mooey sound and went down on her side. The bulls somehow knew what was happening before we did. They were lined up by the fence, Steve as nervous as any father-to-be. Mallory

"We also had to practice walking on two legs."

lowed in pain, but I couldn't tell if she was grimacing or smiling, and then almost as quickly as it began, here it was, the calf, spilling out of Mallory like a small surfer on a small wave, and immediately trying to stand, immediately trying to join life.

It was then I noticed the farmer and his boys watching from another point along the fence. And for a moment, it was as if this little calf had brought us all, man and animal, together. I could see the man smiling. Was that a tear I saw gathering in the corner of his eye? Just for a moment, the moment of birth, I felt like we were all one on the green planet and everything was gonna be okay. But that was just a moment, and moments, by definition, are momentary, and pass. Then I saw one of the boys make a joke about all the gooey afterbirth on the ground, and the bulls horsing around with one another like they'd actually done something, and just like that, the moment was gone, replaced by reality.

And the reality was that Mallory had had a baby girl calf, a beautiful healthy baby girl. Even though I could tell she was dead tired, she was licking the blood and slime from her just as the newborn stood up on wobbly legs. "I'm gonna name her Elsie, Jr.," Mallory said.

It was my turn to cry.

CHAPTER
TWENTY-THREE

IT'S HARD TO LEAVE ANYWHERE

As the sun was going down, Mallory awoke from a long nap, her calf, Elsie, still sleeping beside her. She looked different to me. I couldn't put my finger on it, mostly 'cause I don't have any fingers, but also because it was mysterious. She looked like someone. And then it hit me — she looked like my mother. "Mallory," I said.

ELSIE

I'm leaving tonight.

MALLORY

I know.

ELSIE

And I know you can't come with me, but I'm gonna come back for you and Elsie, Jr., as soon as I figure out how.

MALLORY

No.

ELSIE

No what?

MALLORY

Don't come back for me, I won't go. I won't leave this place.

ELSIE

How can you say that? You know what they'll do to you? You know what they might do to little Elsie. You know about the V word.

MALLORY

I know, but this is the only life I've ever known, the only life any of the cows in my family have ever known. I'm not brave like you. You were made to explore, to discover new things. I wasn't. I know I don't have forever here on the farm before they kill me, and that they will kill my baby after that, but we all have to die sometime and I want what little time I have here to be peaceful, in the pasture, playing with my girl and her daddy. You may not think that's a beautiful life, but I do. And just one day of that life is worth everything to me. Please don't hate me. You can think I'm a coward, but please don't hate me.

ELSIE

I don't hate you, Mals, and I don't think you're a coward. In fact, you are the bravest woman I've ever known.

I meant it. Maybe I was the coward for running away. Or maybe we were just different, cut out for different lives, and each of us was doing what we had to. I leaned into Mallory with all my weight, which is how cows hug. Her eyes closed and she fell back asleep leaning on me. It was night-time now. I heard a rustling at the back of the barn and I looked up to see a pig tottering upright on its hind legs and a turkey with a cell phone, waiting for me. It was time to go. I shuffled over to them.

Just as I was leaving the barn for the last time, I turned around and had this overwhelming urge to stay. Why is it that when we're leaving something is the moment we most appreciate it? My heart was filled with love for all the animals, even the chickens, even the dogs, even the farmers, and I cast my mind back on all the lazy days we'd had — me and my mother in the pasture, Mallory and I talking through the night. So many memories.

But I had to go. When I turned, the pig was looking at me. And he said, "It's hard to leave anywhere. Even if the place sucked. It's hard to leave anywhere at all."

CHAPTER
TWENTY-FOUR

HEADLINE: COW JUMPS OVER MOON
(followed by a pig and a turkey)

It was a nice night, temperature in the sixties, cloudless sky, no chance of rain. Just the sound of my hooves on the grass and the occasional "Oy, my mouth is so dry, does anybody have a hard candy?" from Shalom. We walked in silence for a good long while; I think we must have all been in awe of the moment. "Seventy-five million people, life expectancy, 71.1 years — I'm gonna live to be 71.1!" The gobbler was googling facts about Turkey on the phone — "Did you know that Turkey has been inhabited since the Paleolithic age?" No, we did not. "For the Daily Double [see Trebek, Alex] — does its location at the cross-roads of Europe and Asia make it a country of significant geostrategic significance?" Nobody cared. "The answer is — hells yeah! Go Turkey, go Turkey, it's your birthday!"

Shalom held up a hoof. "Ssshhh, listen, did you hear that?"

We listened — crickets, not much else — and then the silence was broken by the howling of a wolf in the distance. Shalom looked at me, like Oh shit. I said that that howl seemed at least a mile away and not to worry, but inside I was very concerned. It's one thing to hear the baying of a wolf and think it's gorgeous when you're safe inside a locked compound protected by men and dogs, but it's a different ball game when there's nothing but the night air between you and that wild animal. I had always considered myself wild, but tonight I wasn't sure. "Turkey has had a president since 1923, maybe I'll make a run at it." Jesus. "The waters in Turkey are the Bosphorus and the Sea of Marmara — isn't that a beautiful word . . . *Mar-mar-a* . . . *Mar-mar*—"

Shalom had had enough. "Stop with the fun facts about Turkey already. You're gonna use that phone so much, the battery's gonna die and then what'll we do, Einstein?"

"Fine," Tom said, but he couldn't help himself. "Turkey's motto is 'The country unconditionally belongs to the nation.' I don't know what that means, but me likey. Okay, okay, turning it off, powering down."

We walked on, talking loudly about silly stuff to show one another how not scared we were, laughing a little too loudly at jokes, as the howling seemed to get closer and closer. We had covered about two miles, when a shape differentiated itself from the night about ten yards ahead of us, blocking our path — like it had been invisible one moment and the next moment visible, like the darkness itself had taken form.

The form of a wolf. A lone wolf. "Well, well, well," said the wolf, with a wolfish grin.

Shalom immediately soiled himself. "Sorry," he said, "nervous pooper." I had never been in a fight before, let alone a fight to the death, but something told me I was going to be in one tonight.

CHAPTER
TWENTY-FIVE

YOU HAD ME AT SHALOM

"A cow, a pig, and a turkey walk into a bar . . ." is what the wolf said. His white teeth had an unsettling way of catching the moonlight. "Isn't that a joke?" he asked.

"I don't know that one," Shalom answered. "It's not in the Torah."

"I hate jokes, they contain latent hostility," offered Tom.

"Yeah, sure," said the wolf. "I don't quite remember the punch line . . . A cow, a turkey, and a pig walk into a bar, and the bartender says . . . uhh, wait, I remember . . . the bartender says, 'Dinner's here!'"

"That joke doesn't even make sense," Tom said. I could hear his beak clicking because all the moisture in there had dried up in fear. I was sure everyone could hear my legs shaking, my knees actually knocking against each other. "I love that joke," said the wolf, "it's my favorite joke of all. Listen, I can see you all are far from home and out of place, and I have some sympathy for that, as much sympathy as a wolf can have, which is not very much, and I'm not so very hungry, so why don't you, cow, and you, pig, just keep walking and let me discuss tonight's specials with that turkey over there?"

Tom looked faint. I jumped in. "We're on the lam from the farm. I'm going to India, Shalom is going to Israel, and the turkey is going to Turkey. It's a historic journey."

"Wait a second." The wolf held up a paw to stop me. I could see that he was salivating, the liquid running down in thick rivulets from his jowls. He looked at the pig formerly known as Jerry. "You, pig, your name is Shalom?"

"Yes."

"Funny. You don't look Jewish," said the wolf, and he collapsed in a laughter that segued into a horrible series of howls. For all we knew, he was calling his buddies to dinner in wolf-speak. "I'm actually Jewish on my dad's side, changed the name from Wolfsheim to Wolf when we came down from Canada. But you're outta luck 'cause I'm one of those self-loathing wolves."

Shalom couldn't take it. He pointed at Tom. "He's got white meat!" Tom pointed back at Shalom. "He's the other white meat!"

This was going to hell in a handbasket quickly, we were already turning on one another. I knew I had to think fast.

"Look, wolf," I said, trying to sound as tough as I could (all of a sudden I had a New York accent), "we are all animals here, maybe some are a little wilder than others, it's true, but we are all brothers and sisters who have been wronged by human beings — we have been kept and fattened only to be slaughtered, and you, you get shot at and have your traditional hunting grounds unfairly encroached upon by the Man."

I could feel the moment lending me a kind of eloquence. "And if we fight amongst ourselves, then who wins?"

"Me?" the wolf replied. "I would win a fight against you."

"No. Humans win, our common enemy."

"Oh, oh, oh, I see what you mean." The wolf nodded. "Yeah, common enemy." Maybe there was hope, but the wolf continued, "I'm not really political. I'll just take the turkey."

He started toward Tom with that slinky low wolf slide, his eyes beady and merciless. I could see Tom's terrified face lit up from the light of the phone, his wattle quivering in the night.

Out of nowhere, a flash of pink strobed the darkness, and the wolf went tumbling sideways as if he'd been yanked by an invisible hand, letting out a pathetic little whimper. WTF?

Shalom had taken a running start and thrown his entire body weight against the wolf. And Shalom is a fat dude. He's a pig. The wolf was dazed, momentarily off balance, but I could see the pure animal power and need returning to his eyes.

"Okay, for that little move, fatty, you have just become dessert. Every American's fantasy — pork chops and bacon for dessert." The wolf was regaining the wind that had been knocked out of him by Shalom's body block. I knew I only had seconds, so I rushed forward and started stomping on the wolf as best I could. I'm not fast, but I am strong and heavy,

"Out of nowhere, a flash of pink strobed the darkness."

and I could feel once or twice something soft and squishy flatten beneath me.

Now the wolf was howling in pain. I was pretty sure I'd broken a paw or two, if not a leg. He limped off and became one with the darkness from whence he came. I was snorting breath like a bull, when out of the dark, the wolf's voice came again, a lingering threat. "I'll be back, folks, I'll be back with my pack."

With the wolf hobbled, Tom finally recovered his courage and gobbled out, "Bring it on, son, you just got your ass handed to you by a milk cow! This little piggy just made you his maccabeeyotch! Go ahead, bring your friends, we'll tell them you got owned by a proud turkey, a fat little pig, and a moo-cow! Boo-ya!"

CHAPTER
TWENTY-SIX

COUNTRY COW, CITY COW

On we walked, keeping an ear out for the wolf pack. We were getting tired from walking so many miles, but as soon as we saw the tall buildings of the city on the horizon, it renewed us like a good night's sleep. We hadn't said anything for a while. I wanted to lighten the mood, so I said, "'Moo-cow'? Really?"

"Yeah," complained Shalom, "and who you calling fat? I have a slow metabolism. I'm husky, I'm big boned . . ."

"C'mon," Tom said, "I was in the moment, you can't blame me, I'm a free bird, I speaks my mind."

"And what were you doing with the phone when the wolf was coming at you?" Shalom asked. "Were you gonna stop him cold with some Wikipedia Turkey facts, or maybe blind him with your flashlight app?"

We laughed. And walked, and laughed some more to relieve our stress, and when we figured we were about a mile away from the city, we decided to catch some sleep so we could be at the top of our games tomorrow. We took turns keeping sentry. The wolf had spooked us.

In the morning, the plan was to try to reserve airline tickets to India, Israel, and Turkey and then head on out to the airport in disguise. I had memorized the farmer's credit card numbers — Visa and Amex — so I was pretty sure we could charge the tickets. Once we had tickets, the rest would be easy. We could use the phone, and with Tom's beak, we could pick out the appropriate keys.

On a small road just outside the city limits, we stopped and got online. It worked like a charm, and even though Tom pecked the wrong key occasionally, we got it done and had three tickets waiting to be picked up at the airport — one to Mumbai, one to Tel Aviv, and one to Istanbul. (Nonstop! :)) It was gonna work! I couldn't believe it, it was gonna work. We sipped some water from a nearby stream and headed to the concrete jungle.

Tickets were one thing, we could do that without talking. But now we had to figure out a way to get to the airport without being stopped along the way.

Wandering through the actual city, with the asphalt starting to irritate my feet, we spied a man in an apron exit the back of a bar toward a dumpster in the dirty alleyway, dumping what looked like a lot of good food into it, just throwing it away. Like a week's worth of food.

We approached the dumpster warily. A few rats were already in there fighting over the food. They looked at us with murder in their eyes. I said, "Don't worry, good rats, it looks like there's plenty for everyone."

"Plenty for everyone — ha! What are you doing here, country folk? This is rat turf. You won't survive three days here. Welcome to the jungle, baby, you're gonna die!" (*See* Rose, Axl.) And then the little bastard shot at me and bit me right above the hoof and drew blood. I couldn't believe it. He laughed. "You get high?" he asked. This kid was nuts. "I got sense, blow, ecstasy — whatevs you want. You just left the farm for the pharmacy."

My mouth dropped open, nothing to say. He laughed again. "You'll come looking for me. Remember, first one's free." And off he went. He turned back when he was almost gone. "Oh, and piggy," he sneered, "I left you a special little somethin' in there. Buon appetito, hicks."

Now I don't like to judge any animal, and I knew some rats back at the farm who were good people, smart, industrious, enterprising — family very important to them, solid species. So these rats were weird, and the only conclusion I could draw is that's what living in a crowded city stripped of nature does to you, can drive you a little crazy. 'Cause these city rats were real a-holes. Real rat finks.

The three of us went dumpster diving. I was shocked at what people throw away. You could feed dozens of animals with this so-called garbage, half-eaten rolls, rice, good greens. None of it made sense, people didn't make sense, but we were starving so we all just dug in. I was munching on some romaine lettuce when I heard a feeble squeal behind me. It was Shalom. He was frozen, his eyes wide in fear, his lips quivering like a baby's. What? I asked him. What what? But the cat had his tongue, he could only point. There, on a piece of a poppy-seed roll, was a creamy white substance, kind of gross-looking, throwing off some greasy oily color as it went bad. I'd never seen it before. I sniffed it. It smelled pretty good. I licked it. It tasted pretty good.

SHALOM (aka Jerry)
NOOOOOOOOOOOOOOOO!

I stopped in mid-lick like somebody was taking my picture.
SHALOM was trying to get a word out but he was stuttering terribly.

SHALOM
MMMMMMMMMMMMMMMMMMMM
MMMM . . .

ELSIE
Mmmmmmmmmmmmmwhat?

SHALOM
MMMMMMMMMMAAAAAAAAAAAA

ELSIE
Maaaaaaaaaaaaaaaaaaam?

SHALOM
MAYONNAISE! MAYONNAISE! MAYONNAISE!

ELSIE
Okay, it's mayonnaise, what's the big whoop?

SHALOM
MAYONNAISE! MAYONNAISE! MAYONNAISE!

ELSIE

Stop screaming!

TOM *came fluttering over, and nodding like the coroner on a bad TV show, said under his breath —*

TOM

Ah yes, mayonnaise . . .

SHALOM

MAYONNAISE!

ELSIE

What on earth is going on?

TOM

There is a very popular sandwich among humans, one that's been popular for decades, one that incorporates mayonnaise as its customary dressing. It's called a [*whispering*] BLT. [*He pronounced it "blit."*]

ELSIE

A blit?

SHALOM

BLT!

TOM

Well, how to be delicate here? . . . The L and T stand for lettuce and tomato.

96

ELSIE

Fine.

SHALOM

NOT FINE!

TOM

And the B stands for . . .

SHALOM

Don't say it! Do not say the word that shall not be
spoken!

TOM

Bacon?

SHALOM

No, not the B word!

*And he started spazzing out, banging his head against
the inside of the dumpster, trying to get away from the
sandwich. I understood. His B word was my V word.
I guess we all have our words. It wasn't pleasant.
Tom had now taken Shalom under his big useless wing
and was comforting him, stroking his snout.*

TOM

There, there. It's all very psychological, probably goes
back to his mother, that sow, but . . . um . . . acon-
bay.

SHALOM

What? What did you say?

TOM

Acon-bay, what? Nothing . . . anyway, acon-bay is like kryptonite to a pig, that and ork-pay.

SHALOM

What? You think I don't know pig Latin? Pigs created pig Latin! That's why it's called PIG LATIN!

ELSIE

That's what those nasty rats were talking about.

TOM

Relax, I said ork-pay. Anyway, these are certain things that strike to the heart — CRANBERRY SAUCE! CRANBERRY SAUCE! CRANBERRY SAUCE!

Out of nowhere now, TOM was completely losing it, jumping up and down, fluttering madly, his wings kicking up food and gunk everywhere. Especially this gelatinous crimson substance that was so inorganic it still had grooves from sitting in a metal can.

ELSIE

So? Cranberry sauce . . . so what?

SHALOM

Don't you mean an-cray erry-bay auce-say?

TOM

So what, you ask me. So what, she asks. So what.
I will tell you so what. Every Thanksgiving next to
the dead bird, next to the murdered turkey — they
set the cranberry sauce. Cranberry sauce is a trai-
tor. Cranberry sauce is the enabler of Thanksgiving.
Cranberry sauce is the Benedict Arnold of condi-
ments. Cranberries grow in a bog and they should
stay in a bog. What's a bog?

SHALOM

APPLESAUCE!

ELSIE

Oh shit, here we go again.

Now I had a turkey jumping up and down
yelling "Cranberry sauce!" and a pig still fixated on
bacon and newly worried that ork-pay ops-chay
might be lurking near the apple auce-say — all he
needed was a slice of omato-tay to send him
squealing over the edge. And I was wondering if I
was the last animal on earth to realize that humans
eat us all and not only that, they throw most of
us out without even eating us, throw us away like
worthless garbage. I mean, if I'm gonna be killed
for food, at least eat me and poop me out and
let me rejoin the circle of nature. Don't kill
me for no reason at all. And that's when I saw it
— a half-eaten hamburger. And that's when I lost
it too. I started mooing like a banshee. The entire

country was mad and it was making me mad. I thought, This is what it's like to be a mad cow.

CHAPTER
TWENTY-SEVEN

KOSHER KORNER

Shalom was in bad shape. Pigs don't bounce back so fast, not known for their resiliency are pigs. They tend to roll in the deep mud. We had a few hours to kill before we had to be at the airport and we needed to pick up a few things, so I decided we should find Little Israel, the part of town that was heavily Jewish. I thought Shalom might be happy to get a taste of the world he was about to enter.

We found the neighborhood and popped into a clothing store to buy a couple of raincoats and some glasses and hats as disguises. I say "buy," but we actually stole. It was easy, no one expects a cow or a pig or a turkey to steal a pair of Ray-Bans (product placement) and velvet shorts like the guy from AC/DC, so they look right through you and do not see you. People see what they think they'll see and unless you do something really stupid, you can be invisible. Then we went into a bookstore and lifted some books on Judaism for Shalom and a Star of David for him to wear around his neck and a yarmulke for his head.

Shalom was perking up, smiling at the men walking by in the big fur hats and the women in the drab, colorless clothes. He started nodding at folks, and saying "My people!" and "Shalom, brother, Shabbat shalom" and a bunch of words I didn't understand. People took a wide berth around him. The pig was right, these people did not want to touch him. They looked at him like he was crazy, and I'm not sure they were wrong.

A couple of wiseass kids flew by on their bikes, almost clipping us, and Shalom yelled, "You little schmucks!" He started using those foreign words, he called it Yiddish, but it sounded a lot like pig German, and I think he made it up like pig Latin. He spoke this Yiddish at passersby and a strange new accent subtly and then not so subtly took over his voice, like he was from Poland by way of Brooklyn. He said the kids were "meshuga." At one point he yelled out: "Remember the six million!" He started complaining about the "goyim," and that he was going to find himself a "shiksa." I thought, Isn't that a type of razor to shave with? A Schick? (Product placement.) What did I know, there aren't a lot of Jewish animals in upstate New York outside the Catskills.

Shalom started dancing the hora and singing "If I were a rich pig, hamma deedy dada deedy dada dum . . ." from *Fiddler on the Hoof*. When he finished with that, he started in on any Barbra Streisand song he knew, and then it was on to the Neil Diamond songbook. No one seemed to care, though, not even the chair. Then, suddenly, Shalom stopped mid-Diamond.

Cliffhanger!!!

CHAPTER
TWENTY-EIGHT

THE FIRST CUT IS THE DEEPEST
(*see* Stevens, Cat)

"I have to find a mohel!" he announced. "Who?" I asked. We were in high spirits to match his high spirits.

"Not who, what. A mohel is a man skilled in the art of removing the foreskin from a Jewish man's penis."

"Like a penis tailor?" offered Tom helpfully.

(My editor loves that joke. I'm on the fence.)

"Oy gevalt. You are foul. If you must be pedestrian, yes, like a 'penis tailor.' I am a Jew, but I have a goyische schmeckel, and my petzl would like to convert. It is a seal on the covenant between man and God, and I don't feel comfortable going to Israel with a fully intacto schlong, if you know what I'm saying."

(Let me add a note here that my editor says that "the double entendre is the lingua franca of kids' movies." Whatever that means.)

I was uncomfortable with everything he was saying, with this whole line of thinking, but it was clear Shalom was passionate about trimming a certain part of his anatomy and donating it to the glory of his god, so Tom googled a mohel in the neighborhood and there were like five in the vicinity. Who says you can never find a mohel when you need one?

We found the mohel's address. Shalom seemed to lose his nerve momentarily, but then he produced a bottle of Manischewitz (product placement) he must have lifted and swilled three healthy gulps. He invited Tom to accompany him, saying he was sure he could get two snips for the price of one, but Tom said thanks but no thanks. "How long will this take?" I asked. Shalom said, "A good while. See, it takes an hour to mow a small lawn and a couple of hours to mow a big lawn, if you catch my drift." Then he turned on his hoof with bravado and went inside.

"So we'll be back in ten minutes," Tom called out after him.

As we waited for Shalom to finish with the mohel, or rather for the mohel to finish with Shalom, Tom and I strolled the quiet neighborhood. It didn't feel quite as safe without our pig muscle as I looked at some sausages in butcher's windows and then — oh, my mind reels at the thought — tongue, sliced thinly on rye. I got a little light-headed, I could have barfed. Tom was nervous too, 'cause he heard a lot of turkey sandwiches get ordered. Luckily, we had put on our raincoats, hats, and glasses so no one seemed to know who, or rather what, we were.

CHAPTER
TWENTY-NINE

JUST A LITTLE OFF THE TOP

After about fifteen minutes, we made our way back to the mohel. The door opened, and there stood Shalom, a makeshift diaper around his waist and a lollipop in his mouth. If it's possible for a pig to be paler and whiter and pinker than usual, he was paler and whiter and pinker than usual.

"That was quick," Tom said, trying to make light.

Shalom's face was ashen. "My poor schvantz. We shall never speak of what happened in there. Is that clear?"

Tom and I both nodded, stifling laughter.

"Ever," Shalom said, "never ever ever. That man, that man is a butcher! I've seen things. I tell you I've seen things a pig should not see. Things that cannot be unseen. What just happened never happened."

We started away. "Let me get this straight," Tom said, tongue firmly in beak. "Not a word ever about the mohel and the shtupper?"

Shalom, limping slightly, hissed, "Don't say that word."

"C'mon, forget it. It's already such a schlong schlong time ago." Tom was convulsing.

"Schmuck."

"What word? *Mohel?*" I asked.

"Oh, everybody's a comedian!" grunted Shalom.

Tom couldn't help himself. "*Never Say Mohel* . . . wasn't that a James Bond movie — *Never Say Mohel Again?*"

"Enough with the pupik jokes, you putz."

A few moments of silence, then: "Moo-yl," I lowed.

"Zip it!"

"What? I was mooing," I said. "You can't ask a cow not to moo-yl."

"Not funny, guys, my diaper is chafing. You goyim are all alike."

CHAPTER
THIRTY

FLY LIKE AN EAGLE, OR A SQUIRREL

We knew we were getting close to the airport because the planes overhead started getting louder and louder and lower and lower. I noticed Tom was studying them intently, and flapping his wings a little. "What are you doing?" I asked. "It doesn't look so hard," he said, "to fly."

And with that, he took a running start, flapping madly, trying to get airborne. Maybe he got a couple of inches off the ground. Maybe. "You see that?" he said. "I flew!"

"Yeah, yeah . . ." I lied.

"Check this out," and he took off running again toward the edge of a little hill we were on, belting out the old Steve Miller classic, "I want to fly like an eagle . . ."

With that he jumped as high as he could off the cliff, seemed to hover for a moment, and then sank straight down like a stone. Shalom and I ran to the edge and looked down just in time to see Tom hit the ground with a grunt and a thud and roll a few times beak over tailfeather. It was funny the way a cartoon is funny.

Tom rolled to a stop, stood up, and exhaled. "That is another thing that never happened."

"What never happened, you succumbing to the harsh law of gravity?" asked Shalom, tongue in snout. "I see you can dish but you can't take, what is sauce for the goose is not sauce for the gander."

"Yeah, never happened," shouted Tom as he scampered back up the hill. "Like the mohel never happened, like your circum —"

Shalom cut Tom off. "I get it. No need to elaborate," he said as he adjusted his diaper.

"Saw what?" I asked.

We walked on in silence for a while. I could see Shalom stealing glances at Tom, sensing Tom's dream had died a little, and it seemed to soften the pig. Finally, Shalom said, "That thing that didn't happen?"

"Yeah," answered Tom, wary of an attack.

"Dude, I swear, maybe you didn't fly, but you were gliding like a badass," Shalom offered.

"Really?" asked Tom, cheering up just a bit. "Gliding is a lot like flying, isn't it?" he said.

And now Shalom grinned. "Gliding like a goddamn flying squirrel, my avian friend, like a goddamn flying squirrel."

CHAPTER
THIRTY-ONE

A TERMINAL CASE

The airport terminal was very big and confusing, but we knew we had to make it to one of those automated ticket machines. Tom was still in denial. "Maybe I'll just glide myself to Turkey. Who needs a plane?"

I protested. "No, Tom, we need your beak, neither Shalom nor I have prehensile fingers, your beak is the nearest thing we have to a finger, please don't glide away."

"Okay, friend, for you I will temporarily ground Air Turkey."

"I appreciate that," I said as we entered the terminal.

I was so happy our disguises were working.

I'm sure we made for an interesting sight — big ol' me, well over six feet on my hind legs (Oy, as Shalom would say, was my back killing me), in a beige raincoat and sunglasses, and Shalom dressed in the velvet pants of a little schoolboy, holding our pet turkey by the leash.

We had had the foresight to register Tom as a comfort turkey, an emotional-support fowl. There was a program where you could get your dog permitted to travel in the cabin with you rather than in storage to comfort you if you were a nervous flyer, and we were able to get Tom the same accreditation online. He had taken the course on the phone, and had learned some rudimentary therapeutic insights. Which made him very annoying. He kept lapsing into a German accent and saying things like "Zat pig has ein 'edible complex'" or "Tell me about your mother." He told me the pain in my hooves was all in my head, and I told him the pain in my hooves was gonna be all in his ass if he didn't quit it.

"Apparently, you are having some transference resistance. I should get a pipe. Would you respect me more if I smoked a pipe?" he asked me.

Tom's other problem was that the leash made him very nervous and sweaty. Anything around his neck made him nervous, and I understood — his greatest primal fear, one that was in his DNA, passed down from centuries of turkeys that had endured the peculiar American custom of Thanksgiving, was of the chopping block. His neck stretched out long and the blade glinting through the air coming down at light speed, his truncated life flashing before his eyes.

"Shut up!" Tom barked. I hadn't realized I'd been saying that last bit out loud.

"My bad," I apologized as we approached the automated ticket dispenser. Tom continued to tug at the leash around his neck like Rodney Dangerfield in his heyday. Shalom was getting his jollies treating Tom like a dog, saying things like "Heel" and "Good boy!" Referring to the phone, I relayed Tom the confirmation numbers for our reservations and he pecked at them on the computer screen. It went off without a hitch. All our planning was paying off. Like magic, the printed boarding passes slid slowly out of the mouth of the screen, one, two, three — to us they looked like winning lottery tickets, 'cause that's what they were.

CHAPTER
THIRTY-TWO

DOG BITES PIG

We walked over to the big board where they show the times and gates of all arrivals and departures, and as we looked, we could see the flights to India, to Turkey, and to Israel, all on time. It was too good to be true. We each took one of the passports we had stolen from the farmer's underwear drawer, and as we were fixing to say our goodbyes and head to our respective gates, we became aware that one of those bomb-sniffing dogs had become very interested in us, especially in Shalom. Shalom wheeled around and said, "Get your nose out of my butt, dude."

"That's all right, mama, don't fight the law," said this German shepherd with a thick Rhineland accent, even though he seemed partial to American urban patois, which made him end up sounding like Dirk Nowitzki.

"What's your name, sweet thang?" I guess the diaper and disguise were fooling this particular doggy into thinking not only that Shalom was a dog, but that he was female as well.

"What? Did you just call me 'mama'?"

I realized what was going down before Shalom did, and I started urgently shaking my head from side to side, imploring him not to blow our cover while we were so close to victory.

"I like me a feisty bitch," the dog growled comically. "Well, all right now. Look at you standing tall on your hindies — you go, girl. Can I holla at ya? Can I holla? Can I holla?"

I felt for Shalom, doubling down on the indignity of having physically injured his manhood earlier in the day, and now this, a psychic injury to that same ailing masculinity.

"Did you just call me a bitch, Rin Tin Tin?"

The dog kept sniffing the air around Shalom like it was the sweetest of perfumes. "Funny story. I am related to the Rinster on my mother's side. Truth. You ever dated a shepherd? We Germans, well, let's just say we do our business and we take care of business, our clocks are not the only things that run on time, if you know what I'm saying."

"I have no idea what you're saying."

"You want some of this?" The dog now angled his backside close to Shalom's nose. This was not going to end well. "Can you tell they feed me steak? Go on, have a whiff. I would share with you, meine kleine bitch."

This was making me uncomfortable in so many ways.

Shalom smacked the dog on the backside. "What is wrong with you? Can't you tell I'm a pig?"

The dog froze, stopped breathing, his eyes registering shock, disappointment, and embarrassment all at once.

"Of course I know you're a pig. My nose is a highly trained instrument. Not only did I smell out that you

113

"Did you just call me a bitch, Rin Tin Tin?"

were a pig but that you also may be smuggling drugs."
He spoke into a radio attached to his collar. "Code
green, repeat we have a code green, requesting backup."

"Whoa, whoa, wait a minute," I said. "That's not fair."

"And I'm a guy!" said Shalom.

"Now that I didn't get. I have to admit. Are you
sure?" asked the dog.

"Am I sure?" Shalom squealed.

The dog nodded. "Okay, then, I am gonna have to
ask you all to come with me. Is that a turkey?"

"Hey, good for you," Shalom said, "you got one
right."

The dog barked to get the attention of his human
handlers. This was all coming apart fast.

"Wait!" I said. I had to do something before the
humans arrived. "It's clear you are not good at your
job."

"Okay, yes, my olfactory powers were not the
strongest in my graduating class. What are you, a deer?"
he asked, sniffing the air around me.

"Close," I said. "Yes . . . or cow. Deer or cow —
either, really. Some days I'm not sure myself."

"That was my second guess. I knew it. Very similar."

"Listen," I pleaded, "we are all chasing a dream here,
mine is to go to India, the turkey to Turkey, and the
pig, or dog, or whatever you feel like calling him, to
Israel."

"So?" asked the dog, seemingly unimpressed.

"Well, let's be honest," I hurried on, "this could not
have been your first choice of occupation, your nose is
not cut out for this work, if we're being honest."

"You are very perceptive, like many deer. Yes, my father forced me to go into the sniffing business like him and his father before him. I hate it." The shepherd made sad dog eyes, and his tail collapsed between his legs.

"Well, you must have had a dream yourself, didn't you?"

"I wanted to be a seeing-eye dog," he confided. "I wanted to help people, but my father thought there was more job security in customs, so I didn't chase that dream, and now I kinda feel like I'm just chasing my tail."

"That's what I'm telling you," I said. "We are all chasing our dreams and so can you."

"It's too late." He sighed. "I'm five years old, I'm middle-aged."

"Hey, man, five is the new three. You can do it. Look, can you read the departure board up there?"

"I can. Anybody can —" blurted Tom and I kicked him, "— not. I cannot. Who could? No one could."

Shalom said, "No, no, it's so blurry from here, I would need a telescope or something."

The dog glanced up. "I can read it."

"You can?" I said. "That's amazing!"

His tail stirred, went to half mast. "Sure, what do you need to know? India, you say — that's 3:55, gate 31; Turkey 2:30, gate 11; and Israel not till 7:00, gate 41."

We gave him the slow hoof clap of somber appreciation. "Man oh man, you don't have eyes, dude, you have binoculars, lasers." Shalom whistled.

116

I made a show of covering myself up. "Oh no, you don't have X-ray vision too, do you? You can't see through my clothes, can you?"

His tail started wagging so hard his whole rear end was wagging too. "Follow me," he yipped as he jumped onto one of those big golf carts that beep around airports. "They're with me," he barked at the driver, and we all piled on for a VIP trip through passport control and straight to our gates. Forget about Global Entry, we had Global Exit!

The shepherd leaned over to me as he turned on the siren, and whispered, "And maybe you're right, deer. It's never too late."

CHAPTER
THIRTY-THREE

PENNY WISE, POUND FOOLISH

First up was Tom's gate, 11. We said goodbye to the shepherd. He zoomed off in the cart, a new dog. Shalom and I walked Tom right up to the gate.

"Well, I guess this is goodbye," Tom said. "How can I ever thank you? Let me see which is my ticket here." He pulled the tickets out. "Uh-oh," he said as he flipped from ticket to ticket.

"What?" I asked. "What's wrong?"

"I knew that was too good a deal to be true! Dammit! I shouldn't have used Groupon!" He showed me the tickets. "I saw that I could get a deal on three tickets, a great deal, but I guess I got us three tickets all on the same flight. It's my father's fault — he had money issues."

"What?" shouted Shalom. "How am I gonna get to Israel?"

"We can get you a connecting flight from Turkey, it's not that far."

"Don't you travel agent me, you jive turkey! I gotta get to the Promised Land!"

"Okay, okay," I said. "This was a mistake. A really stupid, really bad —"

118

"But frugal," offered Tom. "A really bad, really stupid, but frugal mistake. Perhaps because of a dearth of love from my mother, I have a permanent sense of lack, of not being enough, and this extends to money and miserliness."

"I thought you said your father was the problem," I said.

"Father, mother — see how bad I had it?"

"Please, shut your gob," said Shalom.

"But then again," Tom gathered himself, "maybe it's fate that we shouldn't split up yet. Maybe we're meant to stick together to the end. We all have tickets to Turkey, we all wanna get the hell out. I know I don't wanna end up being dinner tonight and Shalom doesn't wanna be some police dog's bee-yotch — so let's do it. Let's go: Turkey!"

The pig reluctantly nodded his assent. What other option did we have? We headed to give the agent our boarding passes.

"I'd be on my way to Tel Aviv tonight," Shalom grunted at Tom as we made our way down the tunnel to the plane, "if you weren't such a schnorrer."

CHAPTER
THIRTY-FOUR

FLIGHTLESS BIRD TAKES FLIGHT

This was the first time any of us had been on a plane, and while it's true there's not much leg room, especially for a large mammal, the miracle of flight is wonderful to behold. To see the patterns of the earth way below, to soar through white clouds as if they were the Spider God's cobwebs, the bluer blue of the blue sky, the hot nuts — all firsts, and all amazing. When Shalom realized we were traveling on the Sabbath, he got upset for a while, then he claimed he was sure some of his relatives were being served in the ham-and-cheese sandwiches the flight attendants tossed to people like they were seals. At one point he dropped to his knees in front of the food-service cart, yelling, "Uncle Schlomo!" like a crazy person. He finally settled down to watching the in-flight movie, *Babe*, three times in a row, calling out all the inaccuracies.

"This movie is dreck, so unrealistic, a pig would never want to be a dog," he scoffed.

None of the flight attendants gave us any trouble, 'cause everyone acts like an animal on a plane. We didn't stick out at all. Actually, I think we were the most human-acting folk on this flight. The people were disgusting. You should've seen the bathroom.

120

My favorite part was watching Tom look out the window. He'd never flown. And even though he was flying in a metal tube, he was up in the air for the first time. Where a bird should be. For the first time in his life, he wasn't an oxymoron. I could see him flex his wings with the banking and leaning of the plane, the ascending and descending, as if he were the one flying. I saw a tear run down his beak and that made me in turn have to stifle a sob. He saw me see him, and said, "*Marley and Me*, man, this movie always makes me cry. It's got Thanatos, Eros, wish fulfillment, the whole nine." I nodded and went back to watching *Breaking Bad*, season two.

CHAPTER
THIRTY-FIVE

ISTANBUL IS CONSTANTINOPLE

I took a few cat naps en route. I very much enjoyed the hot towel. At one point, a woman leaned over her seat and complained about the service. "They treat us just like cattle up here, just like cows." Like cows, I thought, you mean they're gonna slaughter us and cut us up into unrecognizable segments and eat us? I think not. But because I can't speak, I did the only thing I could do to let her know I heard her. I mooed. "Moooooooo," I said. The lady laughed. "That's right, like damn cows, moooo." I kept mooing 'cause that's all I could do, and she said, "Wow, that is a really good cow imitation." I smiled and lowed, and gave her some of my other cow sound repertoire, and soon she was laughing, having forgotten how pissed she'd been, and, in a bit, she had the whole cabin in on the joke and mooing.

For much of the flight, Shalom studied his Torah and denounced anything he found unrealistic in *Babe*. At one point yelling out, "Bah, Ram, F-U!" Tom, the comfort turkey, strutted up and down the aisles as if he were the captain, making sure that everybody was having a good ride, was being attended to, and felt emotionally "connected." The flight attendant was kind enough actually to let him up into the cockpit with the pilots, where he stayed for what seemed like hours. He came back using all the airline lingo, saying, "I could fly this baby."

Right before final descent, Tom leaned over me 'cause I had the window seat, and we could start to make out the landscape beneath us, the land of Turkey coming into view. The blue of the Aegean, and then the beautiful seaside and dwellings. Tom just sighed and shook his head and said, "There she is. There she is. She is so beautiful. My country." Then a melancholy seemed to fall upon him momentarily, and I thought it might be the sadness that lurks under the happiness of achieving your life's goal — you know that feeling? A feeling like, okay, this has happened — now what? And Tom said, "You know, in France, they thought turkeys were from India so they called us 'd'Inde.' And in Turkey itself, they often call us 'Hindi' for the same reason, and I was thinking maybe things won't be so bad for me if I wanna go to India with you if I'm named after their language after all, right?"

I didn't say anything. I just smiled and nodded. I knew he was nervous about his new life and this was his way of saying he was going to miss me.

Tom's reverie was interrupted by the purser, who came to us with a metallic pin, one of those cheap little captain's bars they like to give little kids, and asked Tom if he would accept an honorary pilot designation and could she pin the little doodad on him. Tom shrugged like no big deal, said, "Sure, I mean, if you have to get rid of them." As she pinned the bar on the bird, Tom could front no more. He wrapped his wings around her and started sobbing. "Thank you, thank you, thank you," he cried, and then, "Do the guys up front need any help bringing this big bird down into the 'Bul?" The purser smiled even though of course she had no idea what the sounds were coming out of his goblet. "I'm just sayin'," Tom added, "just in case things get wonky up there, I'm a bird, mama, I'm here. On the case."

He saluted the purser with his wing, and she understood his body language enough to stand and give him a big salute back while she winked at me. Humans can be decent and understanding at times. Which makes me think there's hope for them.

When the announcement came over the PA system to buckle up for our final descent, I saw that Shalom was sweating like a pig. I thought I knew why. I leaned over and whispered, "I know Turkey is predominantly Muslim, but we're just gonna be in and out of there."

"I'm cool," Shalom mumbled, "it's just I'm a really nervous flyer. You've heard the expression 'When pigs fly'? Well, there's a reason for that — we are not supposed to be up here. I took three Ambien when we took off, but now they're wearing off and I'm out! This is unnatural. Oh geez . . ." He turned back to the rest of the passengers and yelled, "Anybody got an Ambien? Xanax? Oxycontin? A mimosa? I need drugs, goddammit, get me drugs!!"

There was some turbulence, and Shalom squealed, "We're all gonna die! Animals should not attempt to be gods. We are flying too close to the sun, too close to the sun. We're all gonna die!" Tom, the emotional-support turkey, sidled over, whispered to me, "Leave this to the professionals," and took Shalom under his wing. He held Shalom's hoof the whole way down, telling him that the myth of Daedalus and Icarus was not about actual flying, but rather a pre-Freudian Oedipal psychodrama about when man overreaches, and distracting him with aeronautical details and facts about flight.

CHAPTER
THIRTY-SIX

TURKEY IN, TURKEY OUT

At the moment our wheels touched down, Shalom finally fell asleep from all the pills he'd taken. Good timing. Tom and I had to prop him up between us as we left the plane. Tom hesitated at the open cockpit, looking longingly at the complicated controls and lights like he didn't wanna leave. He kept spit-polishing those cheap little wings he'd been given.

We breezed through immigration (go figure), but it took us about twenty-five minutes just to walk through the concourse to get near the outside of the airport. It was daunting and strange to hear humans speaking human, but a different human from what I was used to. They were speaking Turkish, and it was exhilarating, but also a little scary. I couldn't understand a word. I certainly didn't know where to go. Tom had been silent the whole time, and Shalom had fallen asleep and was lying on the floor, snoring and drooling. We weren't going anywhere until he came to and joined the living again.

I went off to see if I could find some coffee. I'd heard Turkish coffee was the best and strongest in the world. How do I take my coffee? Well, the milk looks tempting, but you people pasteurize it and that takes out all the flavor. And what's with this low-fat and 2 percent crap? The fat in the milk is what we live for. You humans are funny, constantly thinking about eating and trying to look like you never eat at the same time.

The Turkish coffee was exactly as advertised. After a few laps with my tongue, I felt like I could sprint for miles and pee for hours. In fact, the call of the cow patty was being whispered to me in Turkish by the magic bean. I had to find somewhere to go. I was aware you humans just don't poop anywhere, and when in Rome, poop as the Romans do, even if the Romans are Turkish, right? I got back to Tom and Shalom. Silent since we'd disembarked the plane, Tom was still staring off into space, head in the clouds. I opened up Shalom's mouth and poured a full cup of Turkish java down his throat. His eyes opened and spun around in his head like a one-armed bandit, landing on triple cherries. He jumped off the floor and screamed, "We're back!" I told Tom I had to get outdoors to relieve myself. He snapped out of his daydream, smiled, and said, "I know just the place." He fluttered up, we followed.

CHAPTER
THIRTY-SEVEN

UP, UP, AND NO WAY

Tom led us back through the concourse, and then through a door that I think said DO NOT ENTER. It was in Turkish so I couldn't really tell, but it was bright red and had lots of warning-type lines through it. I asked Tom, "You sure we're going to the right place?"

Tom opened this door right onto the runway. The sound of the planes was deafening. Tom took off in the lead, flapping away. He ran us up to this smaller-type jet, maybe it was a private plane, and he said, "Let's go for a joyride!" That scared me so much that I gave up all ladylike pretense and dropped a patty right there on the tarmac. The Turkish coffee had the same effect on Shalom, because he quickly followed suit with an anxious deposit of his own.

"What the hell are you talking about?" I asked Tom, screaming over the noise of the planes landing and taking off everywhere nearby. "We just risked our lives to get you to Turkey and you haven't even seen it yet and you wanna get back in a plane?"

"That's just it," answered Tom, his eyes clear, bright, and focused. "During that flight, I realized my home is up there in the sky. Fish gotta swim and birds gotta fly. The prehistoric ancestors of turkeys flew, it's in my

DNA, and when I was up there I felt it in my wishbone. Up there is where I belong. I am a man with no country but the wild blue yonder. The sky is my home." And with that he bounded through the plane's open door. Shalom and I had no choice but to follow him.

Tom bopped into the cockpit, strapped on a headset, and started flicking buttons and running down checklists.

"You sure you know how to do this?" Shalom asked.

"Birds fly. That's what they do. What am I?"

"You're kind of a bird, I guess," answered Shalom.

"'Nuff said," replied the bird, and slammed the cockpit door in our faces. The next we heard from Tom, it was over the PA system, and even though we were the only ones on the plane, he addressed the cabin as if it were a full boat.

"Uh, this is your captain speaking, looks like we are one or two on the runway here, so, ladies and gentlemen, please put up your tray tables and adjust your seats to the upright position. Flight attendants, prepare for take-off."

There were no flight attendants. As Shalom buckled in, he turned to me and only half-joked, "Nice knowin' ya."

The plane was taxiing down the runway, and I don't think we'd been cleared for takeoff at all, because a couple of planes seemed to speed up to get out of our way. Seemed like we were on the ground so long that Tom was going to drive us to wherever he was taking us. As we gained speed, I noticed a fence beyond which I could see nothing but the blue Sea of Marmara and a watery grave beckoning. I closed my eyes and braced

"Birds fly. That's what they do."

for impact. I had done all I could. I'd had a dream and I'd chased it and almost chased it down. I was pretty okay with this being the end. Shalom, not so much. He was lobbing every Yiddish curse he knew in the direction of the cockpit. "You meshuggener putz! You should get trichinosis and die! Of all the ferkakta birdbrained schemes, you lousy schmendrick —" And he stopped, but only because I think he ran out of Yiddish vocabulary.

We went crashing through the fence and over an embankment, nose-diving out toward the water. Three of my stomachs jumped into my throat. I closed my eyes again as water sprayed the windows and, and, and . . . nothing. We tilted up. We were clear and making our way up, up, and away.

After we'd climbed a few thousand feet and my stomachs had settled down, Tom came on the PA system again. "Well, folks, sorry about the ascent back there, just a little mix-up with the tower."

"You're a madman! You schmuck!" yelled Shalom.

"We'd like to offer you a free drink to apologize for the inconvenience of the takeoff. We are on our way up to our cruising altitude of thirty thousand feet. Predicting a pretty smooth flight, but please keep your seat belts on while in your seat in case of unexpected pig flatulence, I mean big turbulence . . ."

"I'm gonna kill you!" screamed Shalom.

"It's about two hours' flight time, so sit back, enjoy, we'll have you at Israel's Ben Gurion International Airport in no time."

Shalom stopped in mid-rant when he heard "Israel," and he couldn't suppress a smile. He looked out the window as if he could see it already. "Israel," he said, caressing the ancient syllables as if they themselves had godly power.

"Is-ra-el," he whispered.

And then he snapped out of it and yelled, "I'm still gonna punch you in the gizzard, you schlimazel!"

CHAPTER
THIRTY-EIGHT

TODAY'S IN-FLIGHT ENTERTAINMENT

Tom's learning curve was steep. He was right, flying was in his bones. Within twenty minutes, he was handling that plane like a seasoned pilot. The rest of the flight passed without incident. After about an hour and a half, Tom came on the PA again. "Folks, this is your captain speaking. Because of the heightened security restrictions at Ben Gurion Airport, I'm gonna take us in at a low angle, try to get in under the radar, so don't be alarmed if we almost clip some trees on the way in. We know you have a lot of options when choosing an air carrier, so we thank you for flying Air Turkey and hope you have a safe journey whatever your eventual destination. Flight attendants, prepare for landing."

As we descended, Shalom looked out his window at Israel rising quickly to meet us with the same rapture that Tom had beheld Turkey. Soon we were barely higher than the buildings. It was scary, but the land also felt so close, just within our grasp. Shalom was davening all the way down and said he had a tingly feeling in his "schpilkes."

The moment the wheels touched tarmac, he announced, "The promised land!"

CHAPTER
THIRTY-NINE

A PIG IN THE PROMISED LAND

Tom made a quick, rough landing and yelled for us to hurry out of the plane. Since we had flown in unscheduled and low on a private craft, it would be only a matter of minutes before we were discovered. We hustled out and just sneaked through a hole in a fence around the perimeter of the runway. We could see the outskirts of Tel Aviv in the distance, and Tom dialed up Google Maps to figure out which way to Jerusalem.

It was going to be quite a pilgrimage from Ben Gurion Airport to Jerusalem, but in a matter of hours, plodding through some dicey neighborhoods and then into the hot, shrubby desert, we had come to an area that had been partitioned by a nasty-looking wall of ugly, gray, graffiti-strewn cement and razor wire. There were spray-painted pleas for change and mercy in Arabic and Hebrew, even English; there was a portrait of Che Guevara in black spray paint and nearby a yellow portrait of Bugs Bunny. Every so often there was a forbidding-looking tower manned by faceless men in full riot gear. It seems this part of this country was split in two — on one side those who believed the name of their god was YHWH (can I buy a vowel?), and on the other those who believed God's name was Allah. Jews

"It seems this part of this country was split in two."

and Muslims. And also Christians. Jews, Muslims, and Christians all with Jerusalem in their hearts. It would be beautiful if it weren't so contentious. They all claimed to worship the same god, they all claimed this was the Holy Land, but other than that could find very little lasting peaceful common ground.

In Israel, the Jews had the upper hand, but they were the minority in the Middle East, surrounded by sea, desert, and a people historically hostile to them. Tom, in his therapeutic German accent, suggested they always "felt like David in ze David und Goliath story, a boy against a giant, their slingshot now a nuclear veapon." The entire region, he said, has a "siege complex" and "Cain und Abel issues." Shalom flipped Tom the bird. "Don't get me started, Sigmund Fraud."

The Israelis built this giant wall to keep Palestinian Arabs out of disputed lands they were claiming for themselves. It reminded me of the fences back on the farm that were meant to keep us animals in our place. There is something in man that loves a wall, but what wall menders and fence builders do not get is that when they fence something out, they are also fencing themselves in. Not one but two prisons are made by one wall. Maybe the prison on the fence builders' side is a little larger, a little nicer, but it's only a matter of scale. China had a Great Wall that kept their enemies out, but also isolated the Chinese within. And that isolation weakened and doomed the empire. There was a wall in Berlin. That did not end well. For the wall, that is. There is a fence on the U.S.–Mexican border, and that's not making anybody happy either.

Personally, I didn't understand. To me, they all looked like people, all part of one desert herd, and to cows, all people look alike anyway. We bovines have a saying you folks might adopt — "Some black, some white, some black and white, some roan, all cows." At some point, we came upon a break in the wall of just a few feet and we absentmindedly, unknowingly slipped through into Palestinian territory.

A few hours after this — or was it days, I can't remember — we found ourselves wandering in a desert. The terrain wasn't fully barren, there was some green — shrub and wildflower. It looked like someone had taken a desert and decided to build a garden, but then got distracted shortly after beginning and walked away, the original Eden maybe. It felt oddly forsaken, this part of the earth that was so hotly contested, and it was difficult for me to believe this is where the Ur-cow stood so many generations ago. I breathed in the dry, difficult air and imagined these were the smells inhaled by our First Father and First Mother. It must have been a hard life with so little to eat and drink. It was a powerful private moment for me. It was also f-ing hot and I was quite thirsty. I asked Tom where we were and what did the map on the phone say.

"Last I checked, we were near the Sharafat mountains. Uh-oh. Seems I got some good news and I got some bad news," Tom said. "The bad news is: the battery is dead. No map. Hey, don't blame me, it's a design flaw as far as I'm concerned. They say the 6G is gonna address that shit."

"What's the good news?" I asked.

"There is no good news. It's just I've always wanted to say 'I've got some good news and some bad news.'"

"Mission accomplished, dumbbell. It's 'cause you wasted half the damn battery playing Angry Birds, you idiot."

"Birds against pigs, broham. Best. Game. Ever," Tom said.

Shalom was hot, tired, thirsty, and as pissed as a wild boar. "We're gonna schlep around in the desert forever, you birdbrain," he moaned. "I would kill for a seltzer. You're like a damn tsuris trap. And don't call me broham."

Wander we did, in what could have been circles for all we knew, keeping shy of the armed border guards, and looking for another crack in the wall where maybe we could squeeze through and get to Jerusalem. It sure was a helluva lot easier to go from Israel to Palestine than Palestine to Israel. Shalom was still stewing, lost in his own bubbly water thoughts and egg cream dreams, when a stone landed a few feet away from him. We looked up and saw what I took to be some Arab children about thirty yards away from us, yelling taunts in our general direction, but specifically at the pig.

"It's 'cause I'm Jewish," Shalom explained.

"No," Tom said, "it's 'cause you're a pig. Muslims revile pigs too."

Shalom raised up and yelled back at the kids, "Have a BLT, suckers!"

"Do you really think it helps to fight hatred with hatred?" I asked him.

"I'm not fighting hatred with hatred, I'm fighting hatred with ignorance — it's a fine distinction. This is how it's done in this part of the world, each side plays their part like actors," he pontificated, and he went back to cursing the kids out in his porcine Yiddish.

Now the initial group of two or three boys was joined by about ten others, and what had been the occasional pebble tossed our way became a full-on fusillade of all sorts of desert projectiles. As Shalom again turned to make his religious stand, a rock bounced off his shoulder. "If I back down here," he argued, "it's like dominoes, they'll just keep coming, and where will it end? Not until they've murdered every last one of us."

I said, "That's totally illogical. And you're gonna get us all killed!" Tom deftly blocked a rock speeding for his head, unfortunately using the limb that was holding the phone. The glass shattered. No more upgrade, no more battery, and no more phone.

Shalom held his beloved Torah above his head and waved it like a flag at the boys, trying to get their goat. A big stone crashed into the nail bed of the hoof holding his Torah, and Shalom dropped it on the sand, cradling his bleeding hoof. Fresh blood dripped on the old book. I snuck behind Shalom and gave him a swift kick with my hind legs to get him moving.

"My Torah!" he yelled.

"It's only a book," I snorted in reply.

Just then a big gob of viscous spit shimmied through the air and landed on my head with an audible plop. I looked up to see a camel staring at me. I'd only seen one in the encyclopedia, but I knew it was a camel, and

139

I was relieved when he spoke to me in a standard animal Esperanto I could understand.

"What kind of whacky dromedary are you?" he asked. "Where is your hump, if you don't mind my asking?"

"I'm a cow from America," I said.

"I'm kidding. I know you're a cow. Cows originated here along with the first civilizations. I've been all around the world myself. I used to model in the States, had a big cigarette campaign, my own brand named after me, even had a day, Wednesday, named for me — perhaps you've heard of hump day? But they let me go when I got too old." He looked like he might cry, and spat again. "Sorry, nasty habit, I'm gonna quit."

A rock landed at his feet. "Name's Joseph, but you can call me Joe, Joe Camel. But you probably knew that on account of my fame and such, the modeling." He whipped on a pair of sunglasses. "Recognize me now?" He struck a pose, lit up a cigarette, and acted as if he were looking at a watch. "I call this: 'Oh Yes, I Have the Time.' Not bad, right? Where you wanna get to?" he asked in between a seemingly endless array of modeling freeze frames that he struck with the precision of an Olympic gymnast. He froze with one leg bent in the air. "This one's called 'Hoofin' It, '97.'"

"Jerusalem."

"Ah," he sighed. "Well, you're on the wrong side of the fence; first you gotta get to and through Ramallah." And he struck a pose where he seemed to be laughing at some joke no one else heard. "I call this one 'The World Is My Oyster' or 'The Clooney.'"

"Joe, I think that's a killer pose, and I'd like to see some more, but do you think you could first help us get to a safer place where you can vogue, where rocks maybe aren't raining down on our heads?"

"Follow me!" he spat, and trotted off nearly as fast as a horse.

CHAPTER
FORTY

ANOTHER BRICK IN THE WALL

Joe the camel led us deeper into the desert to his secret place in the wall where the stone had crumbled away slightly and the razor wire fallen down enough for us to squeeze through to Israel's territory. There were no guards in sight, and just like that, we were back on the Israeli side of the West Bank wall. There would be no more fence between us and Jerusalem. As we kept walking, the villages got nicer and nicer, and the irrigated desert got greener and greener.

"Where you headed?" asked Joe.

"Wailing Wall," Shalom said.

"Ah, tourists," sighed Joe. I didn't know much about camels, but I could tell this one was depressed, his hump seemed deflated. "I never go into the city proper anymore. I hated it when they used to mob me 'cause I was famous, now I hate it more when they don't mob me 'cause I'm not famous anymore. I'm afraid you're on your own." He sat down dejectedly. "These days I just wander the desert so I don't have to deal with the public. Such is the life of a has-been."

I glanced around. Nothing looked familiar. We were lost without a phone, and I was desperately afraid we might wander again into a dangerous area.

"We're never gonna find Jerusalem," moaned Shalom.

"Did you guys see the guy they got to replace me?" the camel asked. "He's got nothing. No charisma. No spit. All he's got is youth."

Tom stared at the camel and then exclaimed, "Aha!" He elbowed me aside with his wing, whispering, "Father issues." He sat down next to the camel.

"You zay you used to advertise for ze cigarettes, ya? Ze Promethean phallic zymbol, ya?" asked Tom, once again sporting a ridiculous German accent.

"Advertise? No, man, I was the whole deal. I was the 'it' camel."

"I zee," said Tom. "Allow me to offer you ze paradigm shift."

"Ze what?"

"Ze shift. From ze model to ze role model. You zold cigarette and you did zis better than anyone, but you know what, ze cigarettes are kaput for your health and kaput for the environment, and you are actually doing ze right thing by not agzepting ze blood money of ze tobacco companies anymore."

(Just got a call from my editor. She says, "There goes another possible sponsor and here comes another possible lawsuit. This is not what I mean by 'product placement.'" She cracks me up.)

"Wait a minute," Joe said. "So you're saying that being good at something bad is bad, and when you stop being good at the bad thing, that's good?"

Tom nodded sagely. "In layman's terms, perhaps ya. It makes no moral sense to miss your former A-list lifestyle. You made ze righteous rejection of ze military-industrial-entertainment gomplex. You used to be ze big part of ze problem, now you are ze small part of ze zolution."

"I'm part of the zolution!" The camel rose to his feet and I could visibly see his hump straightening, as if it were being inflated by an invisible bicycle pump. "Thank you for the . . . what did you call it?"

"Ze paradigm shift. That'll be one hundred fifty clams. We made good headway today, but I think you should probably come back three times a week for the next thirty years or so . . ."

I cut Tom off. "Joe, I know you don't like the fans anymore, but do you think you could be part of our solution and point us in the direction of Jerusalem?"

Joe paused, took a deep breath. "My fans will have to accept the new me. Everybody loves a reinvention. Everyone loves a comeback. I will not only point you, I will escort you."

CHAPTER
FORTY-ONE

AND DID THOSE (PIG'S) FEET . . .
(*see* Blake, William)

There are two holy of holies in this part of the world. For the Muslims, it's Mecca. And for the Jews, it's the Wailing Wall.

As Joe led us into the Old City in the general direction of the Wailing Wall, we walked through some well-manicured residential neighborhoods on the way, and wherever we were, pleasant people sitting in the cafés gave us no smiles and pedestrians got out of our way or muttered things under their breath. "This is a bacon-free zone. It's heaven." Shalom giggled. "Eat me? They don't even want to touch me." He grabbed a menu from one of the outdoor cafés and read out: "See that, no ham, no bacon, no me! Kosher heaven, bitches!"

"But doesn't it hurt your feelings a little to be so reviled?" Joe asked him.

"Sure," Shalom said, "it hurts to be hated by my own people, but it's a damn sight better than the alternative."

Joe spat. "Sorry, bad habit, gonna quit. Really gotta quit the spit. I admire how you don't need the applause

145

of the crowd. I'm learning from you, pig. I have to be my own camel."

I was getting the willies myself and I could see that Tom was too, because, while it's true these people wanted nothing to do with Shalom, my brisket and Tom's reputation as being to die for on rye were still most definitely on the Israeli menu. I was starting to sweat. It seemed like we were just going from wall to wall to wall. Luckily, at least for the moment, Shalom created a kind of treif force field around us and no one came near. I honestly didn't know how he was going to live like this for the rest of his life. And even though universal disgust was keeping us safe at the moment, I could tell Shalom's pig heart was slowly breaking.

More and more people started to give the swine downright hostile looks. I got a bad feeling there was no way they were going to let him near the Holy of Holies. As a response to the evil eyes cast his way, Shalom's favorite rejoinder was "Bite me" or "I taste like chicken," and that amused him to no end. As we moved through the market, or "souk," I could feel resentment building as palpably as when you feel a coming storm in the change of desert air.

A few of Joe's old friends came up to him, nudging him on the hump. Clearly they hadn't seen the desert recluse in ages. "I'm gonna stay here and tell these guys about my conversion. The Temple Mount is that way and the Wailing Wall is just up there."

"To the Wailing Wall!" shouted Shalom.

Joe turned back to us and whispered, "Uh-oh, that might've been the straw that broke my back."

The tipping point. A man across the street shouted, "Swine! Devil! You will not go near the Wailing Wall!" Apparently, pigs were associated with devils in ancient lore. Maybe the cloven hooves? I don't know, but soon there was a growing crowd advancing toward us.

"Jesus . . ." muttered Tom.

"Wrong word," Joe said. "Let's get you out of here!" And we all turned back in the direction we had come. And ran for the desert.

CHAPTER
FORTY-TWO

NOBEL CAMEL

"To the plane!" Tom yelled. "Let's blow this clambake!" Four legs are faster than two, and we easily kept ahead of the angry mob, but when Joe got us back to the break in the wall, there was that same crowd of stone throwers loitering on the other side a short distance away, only it had tripled in size and added some adults. Now we were close to being trapped on both sides.

The Muslims started throwing stones again, and the Jews on the other side, thinking they were being attacked, threw stones back at them. Unfortunately, most of the rocks from both sides landed near us. Now it was Tom's turn to say to me, "It was nice knowin' ya."

For the moment, Joe was able to shield us from the fusillade with his bulk and hump, but some hits were drawing blood. Joe looked at me, his eyes as big as mine, and said, "It feels good to be on the side of good now. Good feels good." He smiled and turned to Shalom. "Whatever I say in the next few minutes — don't take it personally. The personal is political and the end justifies the means. Up with the workers!"

He rose up. I had no idea what he had in mind. He turned back a last time. "Oh, and when I say 'run,' you better run like your ass is on fire."

148

"What is wrong with you people?" Joe bellowed, and though the people couldn't understand him, there is something about an animal in distress that even the stupidest, most prejudiced, most nationalistic human can intuit.

"You Jews inside the fence!" He turned now. "You Muslims outside the fence — why throw stones? You agree so much more than you disagree, but you are blind to your own common ground. You both love the same god and you both hate the same pig!" The stones began to fly at a slower rate now.

"If you cannot come together in love, come together in hate today, against a common enemy, embrace in the brotherhood of pig hatred!"

Shalom muttered, "Say what?" Joe winked at him and spat in his face. "So sorry."

One Muslim man shouted, "That's right! You, you dirty Jews, you hate this pig?"

"Can't stand him," answered one of the more menacing-looking Jews. "What about you filthy Muslims, you detest swine?"

"They smell," said the Muslim.

"They're stupid, lazy, and fat," said the Jew. One Muslim threw a stone that hit Shalom. Joe held us with his stare. "Not yet," he said.

A strong-armed descendant of King David and Sandy Koufax slingshot a rock that clipped Shalom again. Joe shouted, "That's the spirit! Do not attack one another, attack the pig! Man is not the problem! Pig is the problem!"

"I don't think I like you anymore," deadpanned a visibly shaken Shalom. "And you weren't a very good model. You didn't really look like you smoked. Just sayin'."

By now the crowd of Jews had spilled through the fence and was met by the crowd of Arabs circling toward them, affording us a momentary sliver of daylight to see an escape route. But a look from Joe told us to hold. Surprisingly, instead of fighting, Arabs and Jews tentatively shook hands and clapped one another on the back, cursing Shalom all the while. A man in a keffiyeh and a man in a yarmulke locked arms. "Kill the pig," they cried in unison. They joined forces in one mass behind us, aiming their projectiles at us. Mostly they missed, but a stone hit me in the hindquarters. These men may have been devoted to their god, but luckily their aim sucked. They were getting closer, however. Maybe thirty yards away now. And the desert was filled with sharp-edged rocks. They had infinite ammunition.

"Now," Joe said.

"Now what, Einstein?" asked Shalom.

"RUNNNNNNNNNN!"

We ran. We ran like horses, like cheetahs, like the wind. We ran and we didn't look back. I don't know when the crowd gave up chase, it must've been somewhere in the desert. We knew the two-legged ones could not keep up, but we weren't taking any chances. We ran like our asses were on fire all the way back to Ben Gurion Airport.

CHAPTER
FORTY-THREE

MOHAMMED'S RADIO
(*see* Zevon, Warren)

Luckily our little plane was still in the quiet corner of the tarmac where we'd stashed it, and we were able to run to it and board without any further incident. Tom took off in seconds like a pro and banked hard left as Shalom looked down at the country he thought would save him.

(A note from my editor here. She asked me to take out "all the religion stuff" because people take religion very seriously. As a cow, I don't understand that, but I certainly mean no offense. I told you already that Mother Earth is our god, and the only thing that offends our god is waste and pollution, not words and pictures and jokes. I have nothing but sympathy for reverence of God in the abstract. Love of God and life is as natural as the force that holds the planets in their dance. But I'm telling you the story of what happened, my story. And I can't leave anything out. My editor says, "Sugar, there's no way Hollywood will make a movie about a Jewish pig in Israel being stoned by Muslims. Too many hot buttons. Too niche. Too indie. We have to think tent pole. Not Sony Classics. Can't

151

the pig go to New York, you know, and meet a girl? Kind of like *Babe* meets *My Big Fat Greek Wedding?*"

I guess he could, but that wouldn't be the truth, you know? And I certainly didn't want to watch, let alone write, a rom-com love scene between Shalom and the lady of his dreams that he cute-meets on the streets of Soho in the rain.)

Anyway, since we were traveling in — okay, since we had stolen — one of those small private planes, there was a Box God screen on every seatback (fancy), and it played a live television feed. So after we'd had some hot nuts and cold mimosas, we began to watch the news on the screen as there were some breaking reports coming in from the Middle East. Apparently, Joe and Shalom had inspired that tiny group of Arabs and Jews, just a handful really, beyond the common ground of hatred, and the two sides were talking again, with rumors of brotherhood spreading in the region. Who knows — today they embrace in shared hatred, maybe tomorrow they just embrace. Just a beginning, but because it was a slow news day, the networks were making a big deal of it. They showed an old modeling photo of Joe on CNN with the caption "Peacemaking Mystery Model." MSNBC broadcast a shot of Shalom with the caption "Savior Swine." And, of course, Fox weighed in with "Hamnesty????"

"You're famous," I said jokingly to the peace pig.

"Yeah, who knew." Shalom sighed heavily. "I don't know if I could've made it there anyway, don't know if I'm enough of a mensch to live the rest of my life

152

wandering the land like Cain. I think maybe I like to be liked too much."

"Well, I like you," I said. "Ya filthy swine."

Shalom managed a little smile. After a few moments, he added, "I think they're all meshuga."

And then he looked out the window down at the greening desert where he'd fantasized he might find safety and happiness, once again a pig without a homeland.

CHAPTER
FORTY-FOUR

MUMBAI, MON AMOUR

An hour into the flight, the "captain" came on the PA. "Uh, ladies and gentlemen, this is your captain speaking. We are currently cruising at thirty thousand feet in a clear blue sky, gentle winds out of the east at five miles per hour — I anticipate smooth sailing. In about seven hours we will arrive at our final, I said final, destination." Here he paused for dramatic effect. "Mumbai, India." Mumbai, the largest city in India, more than 18.4 million people, formerly known as Bombay, also known as Kakamuchee or Galajunkja. Rolling those magical, exotic names around in my head sounded like a lullaby. Mumbai aka Kakamuchee aka Galajunkja. I closed my eyes and slept the deepest sleep I have had since I was a calf napping by my mother's side.

When I awoke, we were already making our final descent into Chhatrapati Shivaji International Airport high above the Arabian Sea. Now it was my turn to look out the window at my own promised land. I could make out some of the seven islands that are Mumbai. From my window, I could already see it was a land of contrasts, the filthy shanty-towns giving way to gleaming new buildings and high-rises. It looked like the past and it looked like the future — a living contradiction. I felt I had never seen such riches and such poverty, such squalor and such beauty. I started to get a little nervous as we floated down to land.

Wheels touched tarmac and we made our usual getaway out the back of the airport. We were getting quite skilled at that. We began walking toward where we figured people lived, which was not difficult here because it seemed people lived everywhere, like dandelion seeds scattered on the hot, heavy wind. The country was teeming with life, difficult, colorful life. Ramshackle houses that looked like they would be washed away in the next monsoon squeezed next to ramshackle houses that looked like they had been washed there by the previous monsoon. Some paved roads, but just as often, a dusty or muddy trail, which I have to admit I preferred. Felt good to feel some dirt beneath my feet, and Shalom loved himself some mud, of course. Everything was stark contrast here, beginning with the brown earth set against the Day-Glo colors the people favored for their flowing dress. Tom had an eye for some strange, vibrantly colored birds he had never seen before, one beautiful bird in particular. He said, "Oh my, my, is that a *Pavo cristatus?*"

"A pava-what?" I asked.

"The Indian peahen, Good Lawdy, Miss Clawdy. National bird of India. As I live and breathe. Top drawer, A-list all the way. But no female on the planet can resist a private jet. Stand back and watch a master at work." He ambled over to this beautiful, vain bird and opened with "By any chance, are your parents

aliens? 'Cause, damn, girl, you are out of this world."
The peahen squawked, turned tail, and strutted away.
Shot down. Poor Tom, he could fly now, but he was still
a turkey with the ladies. To save face, he paused a
moment, and then yelled after the peahen, "I'll call ya!"
He came back to Shalom and me. "Got her digits," he
lied. "Air Turkey in full effect."

As we approached Dharavi, one of Mumbai's largest
slums and one of the most densely populated areas in
the entire world, I started to second-guess myself —
what if it had all been a lie? Everywhere I looked,
people seemed worse off than animals, and animals
were being treated even worse than in the States. Even
the dogs. Dogs! Man's best friend? They all looked
skinny and mangy and beaten down, and no one was
petting any of them. What if cows were not revered in
this country? What if they used and abused and ate us
like they did in the States? Had I been a fool? Was I
going to die thousands of miles away from my home
and my bones never reunited with the bones of my
ancestors?

My first clue came when we tried to cross a busy
intersection. I stood waiting for the light, terrified of the
cars and bikes, railway buses, auto rickshaws, and
black-and-yellow metered taxis that careened by even
more crazily than they do in the States. I put one
hesitant hoof onto the road and, all of a sudden, the
oncoming traffic halted like I had a Box God wand in
my hand and had just put the world on pause. I looked
to see if the light had changed, but it hadn't. I looked
over into the eyes of the drivers inside their cars, and

"It was true. It was all true. I was a queen."

they were looking back at me with a mixture of love, reverence, and patience. I told Shalom and Tom to jump on my back. (I was back to walking on all fours all the time again — I could be a cow!) I began to cross the street. Not one car honked impatiently, and they waited for me to be safely on the other side before starting up again. A dirty man in rags came and put his forehead on my forehead and stroked me, murmured lovingly, and then went on his way. This would happen hundreds of times in the next few days. It was true. It was all true. I was a queen.

CHAPTER
FORTY-FIVE

SINGH A SIMPLE SONG

I could go wherever I pleased, and no one tried to touch the pig or the turkey while they were on my back. I was given candies to eat, and sugar, which I'd never had — they were delicious. In soothing tones, the Mumbaikar spoke Hindi and Bambaiya to me. I piggybacked Shalom and Tom as we sightsaw. We saw temples and skyscrapers; we saw the beautiful Victoria Terminus, renamed but still a symbol of colonial oppression. "This is it!" Shalom cooed. "We hit the jackpot. This country is cowcentric. We are golden gods!" A little girl came up to me with finger paints and put bright colors on my face, made me up to look like the most beautiful Bollywood movie star. I had to check to see if my heart was still beating because I was sure I had died and gone to heaven.

We gorged on sweets made of rice and milk and were given the softest places to lie down. Even the poorest folk, who had nothing, gave us some of that nothing. I had never seen such poverty, and all in a city with the sixth-highest concentration of billionaires in the world. And yet what the poor had, they shared with me even if they didn't share with one another. Humans can be very generous, though not often enough with other humans.

I had nowhere to go, nowhere I had to be. I just wandered. I didn't need to find a home, because anywhere I stopped or lay down was my home. This was truly and literally my country. When I looked into the beautiful big brown eyes of the people, I felt I could see my own reflection.

I spent months this way, or was it years? It was like that Lotus Eaters episode in Homer. The three of us — eating, sleeping, eating, sleeping, being worshipped. Shalom had put on like twenty pounds in the time we'd been there. Tom finally looked like a turkey the day before Thanksgiving, plump and juicy. Being worshipped felt good, a lot like feeling loved, though not quite, not quite. It was like a wonderful-tasting, rich meal that left you a little dazed and stupid afterward. Nonetheless, Shalom took to saying, "What a mitzvah. I'm happier than a pig in shit."

CHAPTER
FORTY-SIX

THE CHOWPATTY GODDESS

We took to hanging around a cool spot by the Arabian Sea called Chowpatty Beach. I was drawn to it 'cause it sounded like "Cow Patty Beach" to me. It had wide sand vistas and a carnival feeling at night. Shalom achieved a deep brown, Bain de Soleil tan, and said, "Miami Mi-shmami. Who needs Flah-rida?"

Tom learned how to swim. Nowadays, he could fly, he could swim. He said, "I could very well be a duck. I might be a duck trapped in a turkey's body." We were sleepy and stupid with sloth.

One sunny afternoon, identical to all the other sunny afternoons, I spotted a herd of loitering Indian cows. My people. I hadn't realized how lonely I was for bovine company, their feel, their smell, the sound of their lowing. No offense to the pigs and the birds, but there are down-home-feeling things you get from your own kind that are necessary from time to time. I broke into a trot to say hello. "Hello, cows, cows, hello. Greetings and salutations. So good to —"

"Who are you?"

Stopped me in my tracks. Spoken in a tone I had never heard from a cow before, haughty, disdainful, cold — almost human. "My name is Elsie Q," I said.

161

"I've come from America." None of the cows made any move to greet me or sniff me. "These are my friends Shalom and Tom . . ."

"We are sacred cows," the matriarch said. "We are the goddess Prithvi, we are Kamadhenu, we are the source of all that is plentiful, all that is good. The milk for the child, the dung for the crops."

"Right on," said Shalom. "Good to meet you, Katmandu. Katnis. Can I call you 'Kat'?"

"Kamadhenu."

"Eluhenu."

"Ka-ma-dhe-nu."

"You say Kamadhenu, I say Eluhenu. Potayto, potahto, kamadhenu, eluhenu — let's call the whole thing off."

Crickets.

"Sheesh, tough crowd."

I noticed that some of the cows were giggling nonsensically and focused on seemingly mundane things, like a clod of dirt, or their own hoof, or just staring into space and smiling weirdly. They seemed so friendly that Shalom and Tom hopped off my back and went over to hang out with them. I lost track of my fellow travelers for a few moments. That was a mistake.

"What's so funny?" I asked that group.

"We are the silly cows," one said, in a lilting accent you usually associate with surfers in California. I guess laid-back beach culture is the same the world over. "What's up, feathery guy? What's up, fat pink dude?" A couple of the silly cows became fascinated with Tom's wattle, that quivery piece of flesh near his neck. Tom

162

was always a little self-conscious of it, thought it made him look fat. "Check out the crazy skin under this dude's chin — flappa dappa dappa."

The silly cows started to pull and stroke Tom's wattle. "Dude, it feels like bumpy rubber. It's freakin' me out." One of those cows offered both Tom and Shalom something to eat that I couldn't see. It was small and brown, like a lost button. They both gobbled it down. I turned my attention back to the matriarch. She met my eyes impassively.

"Why do you keep company with pigs and birds?" she asked.

"Because they're my friends."

"Indian cows only have other Indian cows for friends. We are goddesses. Only we cows are sacred, we cannot stoop to the level of associating with mere animals such as these. You threaten the whole hierarchy with your behavior."

She was sipping a brightly colored sugary substance through a straw, a small wooden umbrella hanging off the side of her glass, and having her hooves buffed by a little girl. She and some of the other cows had bright metal jewelry around their necks and lovely colored silk sashes tied to them. They looked stunning, like movie stars. But even though the matriarch was my sista from anotha mista, I had taken an instant dislike to her.

"I'm not a goddess, I'm just an animal, we're all animals, just like the pigs, the birds, just like the humans, for that matter."

"Heresy!" the matriarch said. There was a lot of consternation and lowing from the rest of the assembled cows. "You endanger our position. If you show the humans that we're animals, they will begin to treat us like animals, and eat us like animals, the way they do in your godforsaken country."

"But it's not right," I said. "It's not right and it's not fair." I noticed that Shalom had a big poop-eating grin on his face and was staring at his nail bed like it was the most fascinating thing in the world. Meanwhile, Tom was flapping around in a circle like a break dancer, showing off how his wattle wattled for the silly cows.

"Fair?" the matriarch said. "Look around you, where do you see 'fair'? Whoever promised you 'fair'? Your mommy? You talk like a half calf. Grow up, cow. You're a goddess, act like one or be shunned by us other goddesses."

"I'm not a goddess," I said.

"Yes, she is, she's a goddess," said Shalom. "She's just kidding, she's a kidder, she kids, she is so goddess you can't even believe it." And then, for no apparent reason, he broke out in a soaring rendition of Whitney Houston's "The Greatest Love of All." He had a pretty good voice for a pig, but still weird.

"What's up with you?" I asked him.

"These mushrooms that grow on cow poop — 'silly sky' — they are excellent tasty," Tom announced, then broke into the Patrick Hernandez disco classic "Born to Be Alive." He did not have a good voice, even for a turkey. But his rhythm was excellent, pounding out that '70s beat with his drumsticks. The silly cows were mesmerized by how his wattle vibrated while he sang.

164

"Psilocybin mushrooms," the matriarch said, "open the mind, and they grow only in our dung, another reason we are sacred to humans. We nourish their bodies with our milk, our dung is used as fertilizer for their crops, and as fuel, and we even expand their consciousness with our mushrooms."

(My editor called and says she's on the fence about the drug stuff. "Parents will love it 'cause it'll make them feel young and hip," she said, "but then they'll get uptight thinking their kids are being gatewayed into the world of drugs by talking animals."

"Much the way my friend Joe the camel was a cute face, reminiscent of childhood cartoons, recruited to hawk the drug called tobacco?" I asked.

"Oh, Elsie." She sighed. "I guess a big animal needs a big soapbox; you know I love you, all I ask is that you always ask yourself — is it tent pole? Sorry, I got another call here, from a horse, grandson of Mr. Ed byway of Ruffian, who's written a tell-all tale of excess and redemption. Later, babe.")

"I'm seeing colors," Shalom said, "colors that have no name."

"We are all the same, dudes," Tom crowed. "Somebody touch me. No, don't touch me. Lighten up, mama cow, let's talk turkey, owwww stand back, gonna kiss myself!"

"Blellow. Blellow. Blellow," Shalom slurred. "Blue and yellow together, that's a color we need a name for. Coining it."

"I'm flying again." Tom crooned like Peter Pan. "You got me straight trippin', boo."

"Tell the porker and the fowl to shut up, as I will not address them directly."

"I will not tell my friends to shut up."

"Are you Hindu?" she asked.

"No."

"Muslim? Zoroastrian? Jain? Buddhist? Jewish? Sikh? Parsi? Christian? Other?"

"They're all the same to me."

"Interesting story," said Shalom. "I used to be Jewish, but now I'd have to say I'm Hindu. You guys are Hindu, right? I just converted. I am Hindu as hell, Bapu . . ." He snatched the yarmulke off his head and tossed it aside like a Frisbee and tried to get one of the cows to lend him a bindi for his forehead. He started chanting, "Can a, can a, can a brother get a bindi? Can a Hindi get a bindi!"

"I used to be Turkish," Tom said, "but now I am . . . sooooo high . . ."

The matriarch shook her head dismissively. "Then it falls to you, American cow. Are you a goddess or an animal? Think before you speak, for we will shun you from our midst if you answer to our disliking."

"I'm a cow," I said.

"You didn't answer my question," the matriarch kept on. "Choose. I asked you if you were a goddess or an animal."

"I am both," I said.

"Choose one," she said. "Choose one or choose nothing."

"I am an animal," I said. "No more, no less."

166

"You dudes are really harshing my high with all the neg vibes. Have a shroom," Tom purred.

"Blellow," Shalom slurred.

I said again slowly, forcefully, "I. Am. An. Animal."

CHAPTER
FORTY-SEVEN

COMING HOME

It took about twelve hours for Shalom and Tom to descend from the silly sky. But that's the thing, you can't just stay high. What goes up must come down. I had spent a long time dreaming of India, it's true. But I'm not upset that India didn't turn out the way I had planned, didn't in the end match up with my dream India. Without my vision of a dream India, I never would have gone anywhere, never would have had any adventures at all. So I guess it's not so important that dreams come true, it's just important that you have a dream to begin with, to get you to take your first steps.

I have dictated this memoir in an undisclosed location (Jamaica) and I am flying back to the United States and to my home to coincide with the publishing of my book. We're all flying back.

Tom is going to try to officially become a pilot, while working toward getting a presidential pardon from President Obama for next Thanksgiving Day. He is also lobbying for Tofurky to replace turkey as the meal of choice for that holiday. It's a long shot, but he seems to have Michelle's ear on this.

Shalom and Joe have been short-listed for the Nobel Peace Prize for their work in the Middle East, and they

"We're all flying back."

may very well win. But first, Shalom may have to spend a few weeks in rehab trying to ween himself off his newfound predilection for psychedelic drugs.

Me? I want America to hear of my journey. I want you, boys and girls, men and women, fauna and fowl, to learn what I've learned — that it is not right to be reviled, nor is it right to be worshipped. We are not gods and goddesses, nor are we devils and beasts. I know nature is red in tooth and claw. I don't blame Wolfsheim for trying to eat us; that's in his nature, what he needs to do to survive. And I know that a life led like Mallory's can have dignity and sanctity, that you can spend a few good years on a farm, have a child, and then be sacrificed to feed someone. There's a simple, circular beauty in that. I happen to be a vegetarian like all cows, but I'm not naive enough to ask a tiger to forswear meat and eat bean sprouts. We are all animals and we have our place in the womb of Mother Nature. Only man has separated himself from the great chain of being and from all the other animals, and I think that has been to his great detriment, and sadness, and to ours.

I can no longer be part of the herd. I want to be heard.

CHAPTER
FORTY-EIGHT

HOW NOW, BROWN COW?

This is my religion — we're all animals, perfect animals created in the infinite image and imagination of nature. It's a life not without pain and competition and suffering, but it can be a life of dignity and mutual respect. I don't know what awaits me when Tom brings us in for a smooth landing at JFK. A heroine's welcome? The bestseller list? Hollywood? The slaughterhouse? It's funny, because after all this, I have been thinking a lot about Mallory, and that maybe I would like to have a calf of my own. A few years out to pasture with a couple of kids seems like heaven to me right now. But I can't. At least not yet. It was given to me to tell a story and it is my responsibility to tell it. I couldn't live with myself if I didn't.

I'll be landing any minute now to spread the word. Look up in the sky. It's a bird, it's a plane. No, it's three underdogs, it's a cow and a pig and a turkey, and we're coming for you. We have a message for you:

You, me, the animals in the wild, the animal at your feet, the animal on your plate, the person next to you —

We are all one
We are all holy cows
Moo

BY E. BOVARY AS COWMUNICATED TO
D. DUCHOVNY (COW-WRITER)
FEBRUARY 2015

172

A NOTE FROM THE COW-WRITER

It's been brought to my attention that certain aspects of Elsie's story are implausible: that our heroes could actually pass for humans as they make their way around the world; that Shalom could actually find a mohel willing to work his magic on a pig; that Elsie could be a milk cow before giving birth; and, maybe most suspect of all, that all three of their intercontinental flights abroad left on time. I know Elsie; perhaps she is given to embellishment like any good storyteller, perhaps to outright lies like any great storyteller. I was taught in school to "trust the tale, not the teller," and I would ask you, dear reader, to extend this generosity to our friends in the animal kingdom.

Trust the tail, not the teller.

DAVID DUCHOVNY

ACKNOWLEDGMENTS

I want to thank Eleanor Chai for thinking this could be a book and Jonathan Galassi for reading it, believing in it, and helping me shape it. Miranda Popkey for being able to ask a thousand questions but never be annoying. Maria Dibattista back at Princeton. Disney and Pixar for turning it down as an animated film and forcing me to write it out like a big boy. Albeit many years later. My dog, Blue, for being the best dog ever. And. My kids who are my constant audience in my head. Everything I write I write for them as they were, as they are, and as they will be.

SUMMER AT LITTLE BEACH STREET BAKERY

Jenny Colgan

Summer has arrived in the Cornish town of Mount Polbearne, and Polly Waterford couldn't be happier. She's in love — with the beautiful seaside town she calls home, with running the bakery on Beach Street, and with her boyfriend Huckle. And yet there's something unsettling about the gentle summer breeze that's floating through town. Selina, recently widowed, hopes that moving to Polbearne will ease her grief, but Polly has a secret that could destroy her friend's fragile recovery. Responsibilities that Huckle thought he'd left behind are back, and Polly finds it hard to cope with his increasingly long periods of absence. So she sifts flour, kneads dough and bakes bread; but nothing can calm the storm she knows is coming. Is Polly about to lose everything she loves?

HAPPIEST DAYS

Jack Sheffield

It's 1986, and Jack Sheffield returns to Ragley village school for his tenth rollercoaster year as headteacher. It's the time of Margaret Thatcher's third election victory, *Dynasty* and shoulder pads, *Neighbours* and a Transformer for Christmas. And at Ragley School, a year of surprises is in store. Ruby the caretaker finds happiness at last, Vera the secretary makes an important decision, a new teacher is appointed, and a disaster threatens the school. Meanwhile, Jack receives unexpected news, and is faced with the biggest decision of his career . . .

OFTEN I AM HAPPY

Jens Christian Grondahl

When Ellinor addresses her best friend Anna, she does not expect a reply. Anna has been dead for forty years, killed in the same skiing accident that claimed Henning, Ellinor's first husband and Anna's lover. Ellinor tells her friend that Georg has died — Georg who was once Anna's, but whom Ellinor came to love in her place, and whom she came to care for, along with Anna's two infant sons. Yet, after Georg's death, Ellinor finds herself able to cut the ties of her assumed life with surprising ease. Returning to the area of Copenhagen where she grew up, Ellinor finds herself addressing her own history: her marriage to Henning, their seemingly charmed friendship with the newlywed Anna and Georg, right back to her own mother's story — one of loss and heartbreaking pride.

THE WRONG CHILD

Barry Gornell

When a rural village school building collapses, only one child survives: Dog Evans. To his own mother and father, Dog becomes a daily reminder of their survivor's guilt. To the other parents he is a hated and feared emblem of their unbearable loss. Now, seven years after the tragedy, Dog's parents have abandoned him. And with no one to protect him, the broken community's desire for justice soon becomes unstoppable . . .